THE AMULET OF KOMONDOR

THE AMULET OF KOMONDOR

BY ADAM OSTERWEIL

PICTURES BY
PETER THORPE

FRONT STREET
ASHEVILLE, NORTH CAROLINA

Library of Congress Cataloging-in-Publication Data

Osterweil, Adam
The Amulet of Komondor / [by Adam Osterweil;
illustrations by Peter Thorpe]–1st ed.
p. cm.
Summary: When Joe and Katie become actual characters
in a fantasy game, they must battle everyone from a
dragon to the FBI to unite five pieces of an amulet, scattered across
Earth and the fantasy world of Komondor,
that will restore everything to normal.
ISBN 1-886910-81-2 (alk. paper)
[1. Fantasy games–Fiction. 2. Computer games–Fiction.
3. Magic–Fiction. 4. Humorous stories.] I. Thorpe, Peter, ill. II. Title.

PZ7.O846Dr 2003

[Fic]–dc21   2002192748

CONTENTS

We Play Our Favorite Fantasy Game	9
We Buy Something Very Strange from Aidan	17
We Play the Coolest Computer Game Ever	26
We Explore Komondor	36
The Computer Game Brings Trouble	43
I Encounter Evil at the Supermarket	47
I Duel a Thief	53
We Explore a Creepy Castle	62
Cartoons in the Real World	74
Captured!	79
We Attempt Two Daring Escapes	85
Eryn Learns Her True Destiny	95
On to the Land of Snowy Mist	106
We Make a Great Discovery	116
We Cross the Peaks of Doom	123
The Garden of Nightmares	129
We Meet Prince Kivin	140
We Head for the Northern Kingdom	147
We Battle an Ancient Dragon	154
We Complete the Amulet	163
Peace Is Restored	171

For the children of Springs

WE PLAY OUR FAVORITE FANTASY GAME

The English Golem arrived twenty minutes before recess. He lifted up a corner of the roof and peeked into Mr. O's classroom, where I sat paralyzed by boredom. The beast was made of ice and stone, and snot dripped from his apelike nose.

"Joe, do something!" Katie demanded as all the kids except me screamed and jumped under their desks.

"Very funny—enough about my bad hair day already," Mr. O said impatiently, oblivious to the giant creature that hovered over him. "Get back in your seats!"

The golem cracked off a giant section of roof and tossed it into the nearby trees. I tried to reach for my DragonSword, but the overwhelming boredom had fused my arms to the desk!

"Joe, what are you waiting for?" Katie pleaded, crouching behind me.

The golem grabbed Mr. O by the collar and lifted him up, emitting a gravelly laugh. Mr. O screamed when he saw the tremendous mouthful of crooked teeth.

"You tells me word dat have no vowels, and me not eat you," the English Golem bellowed. "And dat means no y's too."

"'Cwm'!" Mr. O responded, desperately trying to free himself from the golem's clutches. "'Cwm' has no vowels!"

"'Cwm' funny word. What it mean?" The golem scratched his hairy head.

"It's a steep crater in a mountain," Mr. O said nervously, swaying back and forth. "Now let me go!"

"Har har! If you know dat, den you gud English teacher and you tasty," the golem cackled, lifting Mr. O above his head.

I tried to reach my DragonSword with my mouth, but it was too late. The golem tossed Mr. O in the air and swallowed him in one gulp. Moments later the beast went cross-eyed and coughed until Mr. O's tie popped out of his mouth and landed in a puddle of brown saliva. Then, sniffing the air, the golem set off to find another school and another tasty English teacher.

"Joe, move!" Katie said. "We're going to get in trouble!"

I looked around the classroom. The roof was intact, Mr. O was still here, and all the students sat in groups playing Scrabble. My arms weren't stuck. It had all been a daydream!

"Try to use some of the unusual words that I just went over," Mr. O told the class. He always lets us play Scrabble on Friday before recess.

Katie and I threw a lot of words on the Scrabble board to make it look like we'd played. Then we took out our favorite game—*DragonSteel*.

"I'm gonna win the Red DragonEye from you today," Katie vowed, shuffling her giant stack of cards.

"You'll never get it," I said, picking cards out of

my pile. "I'm too good at defense."

DragonSteel is a fantasy card game with Japanese-style artwork—all the cartoon characters have huge puppy-dog eyes, big spiky hair, and a tiny nose and mouth. The game is set in the magical land of Komondor, where a struggle for supreme power has raged for many years. The goal is to become more powerful by winning cards from other players. There are six types of cards: treasure, equipment, monsters, characters, spells, and amulet pieces.

The only way to win the game is to acquire all five pieces of the DragonSteel Amulet. The base of the amulet is a dragon's head carved from steel, with four empty slots to hold the amulet gems—a red ruby and a blue diamond as the eyes, an orange sapphire in the shape of a breath of flame, and a black opal for a nostril. The company distributed only a few hundred cards representing each amulet piece, so it's hard for anyone to win. After two years of nonstop playing with dozens of kids, Katie has four DragonSteel Amulet pieces and I have the remaining one.

"What are you two doing?" Mr. O asked, walking over to us. "Are you playing that card game again?"

"We're done with Scrabble," Katie explained, pointing at the board.

"Did you actually play any of these words?"

Mr. O asked, eyeing the Scrabble board suspiciously. "Some of these don't look real. What does TAXAR mean?"

"He's a superhero that collects money for the government," I said confidently.

Mr. O kept us in for recess. I didn't get mad because I felt bad that the golem ate him earlier. Anyway, Mr. O was so busy grading essays that Katie and I snuck in a game of *DragonSteel*.

"OK, I'm playing four cards," I said, placing them face up on the table. "In front, the English Golem comboed with a Wand of Ice Shards. Behind him, Warrior Ignatia comboed with a DragonSword."

"Monsters and weapons—that's a typical boy move," Katie scoffed. "Well, I'm playing only three

cards." She slammed her cards dramatically on the table, which made Mr. O look up from his papers for a moment.

"Who's that?" I asked, pointing at a card labeled "Michael Bottompockets." It showed a picture of a masked boy wearing black clothing.

"He's a boy thief. Only fifty of these cards exist in the whole world—I won it from my cousin Natalie, who won it from her friend from Australia. I'm comboing Michael Bottompockets with the Bag of the Grumpy Ancients and a Primitive Torch."

"Bring it on," I said confidently. What good were a bag and a torch against an armed golem?

"Ha! I comboed Michael with a magical bag, so he gets two unrestricted steals," Katie said. "That means I can automatically take any two of your cards, even ones in your stack."

"No way!" I protested.

"It says so right here on the back of Michael's card," Katie said, pointing at the tiny instructions.

"That's not fair!"

"I'm taking the wand for my first card," she said, swiping my golem's weapon. "And for my other card I want the Red DragonEye from your stack of cards. That's the last amulet piece I need."

"Forget it!" I said, way louder than I meant to. I looked cautiously up at Mr. O, but he was asleep at his desk. He must have tried to read *my* essay.

Katie reached for my stack of cards, but I yanked them away and held them above my head. She tickled me under my arm, making me drop all the cards into a heap on the floor. Then she grabbed the Red DragonEye and added it to her pile.

"Now I'm gonna melt your defenseless golem with my torch," Katie said gleefully. She really knows how to rub it in.

"I'm not playing with you anymore," I declared, piling up my remaining cards.

"Fine, I won the game anyway," Katie gloated. "I have all five amulet cards now."

"Yeah, whatever."

Katie carefully piled up the five cards—the Amulet Base in the shape of a dragon's head, the Red DragonEye, the Blue DragonEye, the Orange DragonFlame, and finally the Opal Nostril. Most kids don't have even one of these cards. Most kids have never even *seen* one of these cards. I almost calmed down enough to be a little proud of Katie. After all, my girlfriend could be the first kid to have pieced together the amulet. I didn't mind the sound of that too much.

Then it happened.

The glowing red words "GO TO THE MALL LATER" magically appeared on the top card in

Katie's hand. Before I could examine the card closely, it changed back into the Opal Nostril.

Katie and I gave each other a confused look while Mr. O snored.

"They probably want us to buy more *Dragon-Steel* cards or something," I said. "It's just a marketing trick."

We wondered about this for a while. Then we packed up all our stuff, shut off the lights, and went outside for the rest of recess.

WE BUY SOMETHING VERY STRANGE FROM AIDAN

What mysterious relics have you uncovered lately?" Katie asked my mom later that day.

My parents are archaeologists. Three years ago we moved to Springs, Long Island, because they were hired to create a replica of the Acropolis as a tourist attraction on top of Springs Hill. The Acropolis was a bunch of buildings that sat on a rocky outcropping in ancient Greece. Katie thinks Mom and Dad are Indiana Jones cool.

"We haven't excavated in years because of the Acropolis project," Mom answered, flipping through a phone book. "Lately I've been researching the composition of paint that once covered the metopes and triglyphs of the Parthenon's entablature. Fred's at the lab analyzing some paint chips sent over from Athens, and I've been spending the day scouring ancient texts for descriptions of artwork. But there's one book that I can't seem to ..."

We snuck off to my room while Mom went on about the paint. I have a serious collection of fantasy posters on my walls: *The Hobbit, Lord of the Rings, NeverEnding Story, Everquest, DragonBall Z,* and lots of others. Everything outside my room is uncool: ancient Greek rocks, statues, and a million books about what things were like a long time ago. Even the ancient Greek people would rather be in my room, I know it.

"Wow, you got some new stuffed animals," Katie said, picking up a couple of my bears. "Who are these guys?"

"Snuffles and Koala Bear 3," I said. "Snuffles is a polar bear, but he doesn't like the cold."

"You're the only junior high boy who collects stuffed animals," Katie said. "That's so cute."

"I'm not collecting, I'm rescuing," I said, embarrassed. "It's different." I don't like to let any stuffed animals go in the garbage, not after they loved some kid their whole life. Whenever I hear that one is going to be thrown out, I take it and add it to my pile. The heaps of animals are starting to obstruct my view of the fantasy posters, but I'm attached to the little guys now.

"Joe, do you want to go to the mall?" Mom called from downstairs. "That book I need is there. Katie can come. We'll go to Burger King for dinner."

"Yuck," I said to Katie. "My mom always forgets that I'm a vegetarian."

"The mall!" Katie blurted. "The card *said* to go to the mall."

"It's just a coincidence," I told her. "Everybody goes to the mall sooner or later."

"C'mon," Katie urged, pulling me out the door. "Something weird's going on."

On the way to the mall, Mom's cell phone rang. I knew it was bad news when she kept saying, "Oh, really? Is that so?" into the phone. She was very upset by the time she hung up.

"That was Mr. O," Mom said angrily. "He says you have a smart mouth, Joe."

"It's not just my mouth, it's *all* of me," I whined. Katie giggled.

"He said you goofed off in class, and then you skipped out on recess detention. Is that true?"

"We were just playing Scrabble," I said. "That doesn't count as classwork."

"You do whatever you're told to do," Mom said sternly. "Well, you can forget about Burger King now."

"Good, I don't want a poor dead cowburger anyway," I said stubbornly.

"And no buying any fantasy toys at the mall,"

Mom added. "This insubordinate behavior has got to stop!"

When we got to the mall, Mom gave me twenty bucks for dinner at the Tofu Hut. I guess she forgot that this wasn't a very good punishment for a vegetarian. Then she went into the bookstore, leaving me and Katie to wander around by ourselves.

"What's that place?" I asked, pointing at a shop with a sloppy, hand-painted sign: AIDAN'S CURIOSITIES.

"Let's check it out," Katie said. "It must be new."

We walked into a dingy store full of cobwebs and piles of colorful merchandise. Crowded shelves hung at angles on the wall. One package read "Your Complete Guide to Every UFO That Ever Landed." Another read "Secrets of the Greek Acropolis, Including Never-Before-Seen Ancient Photographs and Unused Vials of Entablature Paint." A small box was labeled "The Everything Box! Make a Wish, Press the Button, and Your Wish Comes True!"

Suddenly a loud crash came from the back of the store. A heap of packages fell over, followed by a banging sound. A small boy appeared between the piles, swinging a broom frantically. He wore giant gag sunglasses, a top hat, a scarf, and a long overcoat. He cleared a path through the boxes and walked over to us.

"Sorry, there're some toxic rats here," he said, adjusting his hat. "I got one of 'em with the broom. I'm Aidan. Welcome to my shop." He looked about ten years old.

"This is your shop?" Katie asked. "Aren't you too young to have a store?"

"Um, well, it's my dad's," Aidan said nervously. "He's also named Aidan."

"How much is all this cool stuff?" I asked, picking up a dusty book called *How to Cure Any Disease Using Only Household Items*.

"I'm still organizing stuff," Aidan said, swiping a pile of junk off the front counter with his broom. "So each thing is twenty bucks for now. Hurry up and choose something, I have to close soon."

"What do you recommend?" Katie asked.

"I just got something in from Japan," Aidan said. "I think it's at the bottom of this pile." He kicked over a teetering heap of crates, swatted some bright yellow cockroaches away with his broom, and picked up a shiny box. "It's *DragonSteel*—the computer game."

"What?" I said as my heart started beating rapidly. "There's no such thing!"

"It's brand-new," Aidan said. "They released it only in Japan, but I have connections. I mean, my dad does, of course. Are you going to buy it or not?

I have to close!"

I grabbed the twenty bucks out of my pocket and handed it to Aidan.

"You better be careful with this game," Aidan said. "It has a terrible problem, a bad one, and I mean really, really bad. Don't lend it to anyone. Heed my warning. It's cursed. Oh yeah, here's a bag."

"What's wrong with it?" I asked, staring at the shiny metallic box in amazement. The words "Revolutionary New 3D Graphics Engine!" spanned the bottom of the cover.

"It's really addictive," Aidan warned, stumbling over to his disorganized counter. "You *won't* be able to stop playing until you win." He stuffed the twenty bucks into a purple sneaker and disappeared behind a stack of boxes.

As we left Aidan's store, he shouted, "Beware— beware of the game! You better listen to me!" We walked faster to get away from that weird kid until we bumped into my mom.

"Mom, you have to check out that place, there's stuff you need in there." I pointed behind me toward Aidan's store, but when I turned around to look, I saw that it was no longer there! In its place stood a store called CLAUDIA'S COMFORTS—FINE UNDERWEAR FOR WOMEN. A sign on the window read "Look! Half Off Bras!"

"What?" Mom said, staring at my bag in a puzzled way. "What's in that bag? Didn't I tell you not to buy anything?"

"But Mom—"

"Give me the bag," she said in a very serious tone.

I held it behind my back so that she couldn't grab it.

"You're grounded for the weekend, young man," she decreed. That was her way of saying she didn't want to make a scene at the mall. I looked around and realized that everybody was already staring at us. Embarrassed, I hid the bag under my shirt and slumped my head.

We had a pretty awkward ride home. Katie and I sat in the back seat and whispered about all the strange stuff going on. The words on the card, the mysterious new computer game, the disappearing store. Had we stumbled into the Twilight Zone?

"This is too weird," Katie mumbled, staring at the game's shiny box.

WE PLAY THE COOLEST COMPUTER GAME EVER

*T*wo shadowy figures wearing leather hats held torches on a stormy night. Lightning crashed around them as they uncovered the entrance to an ancient underground vault. After Fred pried the door open, he thrust in his torch, revealing archaic Greek writing on the wall that read "Take baby or be cursed. Raise him." An arrow pointed down to a basket containing a living baby boy. Fred looked at Patricia in horror.

I sat on the stairs and daydreamed, wondering if that was how Mom and Dad got me. I know they love me, but I don't have anything in common with them, and everything I do stresses them out. Mom sent Katie home as soon as we got back from the mall, and now I was waiting for Dad to get home from the lab.

"We have a problem," Mom said to Dad when he walked in the door.

They whispered for a while. I could make out only the words "Claudia's Comforts," "underwear," and "twenty dollars." Then they got louder.

"Teenagers do weird things," Dad said.

"You told me he wouldn't become a teenager until *next* year!" Mom complained.

"What about that island?" Dad asked nervously. "Isn't there some island where you can temporarily put boys his age? You once showed me a journal article about it."

"That was Joe's book report on *Lord of the Flies!*" Mom shouted. "And those boys started hurting each other!" Dad began pacing.

I ran into my room, slammed the door, and buried myself in my pile of stuffed animals. Snuffles cuddled with me until I fell asleep.

I woke up under the covers in the morning, thinking my bears must have carried me onto my bed. The stream of sunlight on my computer reminded me that it was time to play the computer game. Mom and Dad were away at the Acropolis project, so I called Katie.

"Come over," I said.

"Aren't you grounded?" Katie asked.

"I'm not leaving the house, it's OK. Come on."

I picked up the computer game. Tiny print on the side of the box read "Requires a CD drive and a *lot* of memory." I tore it open, hoping my old computer was good enough. There were no instructions inside, just a shiny CD labeled "I. SCHLEPP."

When Katie arrived, I stuck the CD in the drive and turned the computer on. At once, my house disappeared and we were standing on a glass platform in the middle of a bright blue sky. Katie looked at me, astonished. Moments later we floated into the air and soared over snowy mountains, giving us a bird's-eye view of the cartoon world that I'd always imagined when we played the card game.

"Uh, welcome to *DragonSteel*," Aidan's voice boomed from somewhere. "Long ago in the world of Komondor, there lived an emperor who ruled a peaceful kingdom. This land was once filled with meadows and valleys where playful dragons romped. But one day an evil sorceress named Brucella discovered that the ancient dragons contained a magical energy that could be harvested. One by one she turned the great dragons into steel. When she combined the DragonSteel with certain enchanted jewels, a mysterious power emerged."

We zoomed across a sparkling sea, whose calm surface transformed into the images that Aidan was describing.

"Brucella's ultimate creation was the Dragon-

Steel Amulet. She carved a dragon's head out of the magical steel and attached four enchanted jewels to it: a red ruby and a blue diamond as the eyes, an orange sapphire in the shape of a breath of flame, and a black opal for a nostril. According to the Great Prophecy, when a magical phrase is recited, the amulet's owner transforms into the most divine creature in the universe—one that can control legions of people with merely the blink of an eye. But before she could ever use the amulet, the sorceress was captured and imprisoned by the emperor's army. Then the emperor scattered the pieces of the amulet across two worlds—Komondor and Earth—so nobody could ever wield its power."

A giant book entitled *The Great Prophecy* appeared, flapped its covers like wings, and fluttered around us.

"Now, thousands of years later, Komondor is full of violence. Three evil emperors are fighting for control of the land. Each is trying to piece together the ancient DragonSteel Amulet and use its power to conquer the others. But the Great Prophecy says that only Earthlings can successfully reassemble the DragonSteel Amulet—all others will fail. Your job, brave adventurers, is to reunite the amulet pieces and use its power to restore harmony to our world. Uh, just a second, I have to go to the bathroom."

After Aidan's voice had stopped, the giant book opened and displayed the parts of the prophecy that he had described.

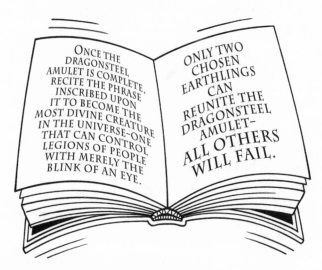

ONCE THE DRAGONSTEEL AMULET IS COMPLETE, RECITE THE PHRASE INSCRIBED UPON IT TO BECOME THE MOST DIVINE CREATURE IN THE UNIVERSE—ONE THAT CAN CONTROL LEGIONS OF PEOPLE WITH MERELY THE BLINK OF AN EYE.

ONLY TWO CHOSEN EARTHLINGS CAN REUNITE THE DRAGONSTEEL AMULET— ALL OTHERS WILL FAIL.

"Are we dreaming?" Katie asked, reaching out to touch the book. It immediately slammed shut and vanished.

"I guess this is what they meant by 'Revolutionary New 3D Graphics Engine'!" I cried as we soared over a thick forest.

"OK, I'm back," Aidan's voice blared from the sky. "There are ten characters to choose from—just let me know when you like one of 'em."

"Let's choose fast," I said. "I want to check out the game, and we can always start over later."

Soon we were hovering over a Japanese-style

cartoon girl wearing baggy pants and a white sash tied around her head. She had tall blond hair and giant eyes, and she was practicing swordplay next to a gurgling stream at the edge of the forest.

"Ignatia, daughter of the Emperor of the West, is famous throughout Komondor for her beauty. Dissatisfied with the stuffy life of royalty, she ran away from home to become a warrior, and now she wanders the countryside in search of adventure. She starts with a DragonSword and a magical backpack that has unlimited space."

"I'll take her," Katie said.

"Good choice," Aidan's voice boomed. "One moment, please."

A crack of thunder sounded. The girl by the stream looked up in confusion and then disappeared. Seconds later, Katie transformed into Ignatia. When she batted her giant eyelashes at me, I did a loop in the air. Was I dreaming? Could this be some new technology Japan had just discovered?

We zoomed across the forest and over the snowy mountains until we hovered above a dilapidated yellow cabin at the edge of a large crater. On the ground nearby, a cartoon boy wearing a bright purple robe sat writing in a book. The boy had colossal spiked hair and giant eyes, and his nose and mouth were barely visible. He looked angry.

"JuJu is rumored to be a distant descendant of Brucella, the evil sorceress. He lives the life of a hermit in the Peaks of Doom, secretly practicing dark magician's magic. He starts with a spell book containing three beginner spells."

"Gimme him," I said. "I wanna get started."

"You sure you don't want a warrior?" Aidan's voice echoed. "Some good ones are coming up."

"I just want to play," I said, flipping impatiently in the air. "I can't believe this is real!"

After another crack of thunder, the boy on the ground disappeared, and I transformed into JuJu. Everything around me suddenly seemed brighter. My tiny mouth could open to the size of a grapefruit! My skin was the color of a peach! Katie giggled as I tightened the belt on my bright purple robe.

We soared away from the mountains and back across the forest until we landed on a rocky hill under the bright midday sun. A peach-skinned Aidan stood next to a pile of discarded clothes—a top hat, scarf, gag sunglasses, and overcoat. Aidan was a cartoon too! Now that he had removed his disguise, he was wearing bright orange shorts and a yellow T-shirt, and his spiky hair was pointing in every direction.

"Who are you, anyway?" I asked. "Are you playing the game also?"

"I'm the narrator, duh," Aidan responded, his giant eyes narrowing in anger.

"But I thought you worked in that shop," Katie said.

"That's my other job. Times are tough," Aidan said, handing us our gear—a black spell book for me, a DragonSword and a backpack for Katie.

"Follow this trail down to the commoners' village, where you'll begin your journey," Aidan instructed. "I'll come by to narrate sometimes. Look carefully at everyone you meet—all evil creatures have bar codes on their skin. Y'know, those black-and-white-striped symbols that are on the back of every book. A DragonSword can be activated only by swiping it over the bar code. Then the sword can harm only that beast—it's a safety feature. Good luck, brave adventurers!" Aidan waved his hand and disappeared.

"Nobody is *ever* going to believe this," Katie said, examining her DragonSword. A shrink-wrapped box contained a fancy metal sword handle with no blade. Big letters on the box read "Safe for all ages! Works only against evil monsters! Just swipe the handle across the beast's bar code to activate!"

"C'mon," I said, pulling Katie along the path. "This is so cool!"

WE EXPLORE KOMONDOR

Katie and I wandered down the hill as butter-flies fluttered around us. The colorful cartoon world felt peaceful, and it seemed odd that anything could be wrong here. When a green butterfly landed on my arm and smiled at me, I yelped in surprise. It flew into the air and giggled with the others.

We soon came to a bustling town where villagers sang as they worked and children chased each other around. As we neared the gate, a round crea-ture jumped into our path, shouting, "Gromlox! Gromlox!" It had two horns sticking out of a wart-ridden head, and a giant bar code stretched across its stomach. It growled as if it had no intention of letting us pass.

"Oh, it's only a lowly gromlox," Katie said confi-dently as three purple spheres appeared in the air.

I tried to walk around the creature, but it sent an electrical charge into me with its horns. I flew

back into Katie, and the purple sphere above my head became slightly smaller.

"Use your DragonSword!" I yelled, amazed that I didn't feel any pain.

"I didn't take it out yet!" Katie yelled back, trying to rip open the box.

"Gromlox! Gromlox!" The creature charged us with its horns, zapping Katie and me into the bushes. The purple spheres above our heads shrank until they were barely visible, and I panicked at the thought of the words "GAME OVER."

"Use a spell—hurry!" Katie said, trying to untangle herself from a vine.

I quickly examined my dusty spell book. The entire thing was blank, except for some old-fashioned writing and illustrations on the first few pages. I had only three spells: *Reveal Truth*, *Divide and Conquer*, and *Divine Intelligence*. With no time to read, I touched the page labeled *Divine Intelligence*. My finger turned blue momentarily, and then I pointed at the gromlox.

"Good day, friends," the gromlox said. "Sorry about that electrical horn business before. There you were happily walking along a path—I dare say that's not a crime—only to be badgered by the likes of me and these menacing horns. Well, we can't quite maintain a civilization if we insist on treating each other like *that*, can we? I'll just run along now." It wandered off toward the commoners' village, reciting Shakespeare's *Romeo and Juliet* backwards: "Romeo her and Juliet of this than woe more of story a was never for ..."

Suddenly the gromlox stopped, turned around, and looked at us with an evil expression. Then it ran toward us like a runaway train, shouting, "Gromlox! Gromlox! Gromlox! Gromlox!"

"The spell wore off," Katie observed. "Cast it again!"

"Oh, great—I think each spell works only once!" I said as I stared at the big red X that had just appeared across the first page of my spell book.

Just before the speeding creature hit us, I cast *Divide and Conquer*, turning the gromlox into dozens of tiny gromloxes that impacted Katie and me like harmless meteors. They each shouted "Gromlox!" in a high-pitched voice and then disappeared into the bushes.

"Congratulations," Aidan's voice said from somewhere. "You've almost gotten a PowerUp Bonus already. You get them by exploring Komondor, defeating monsters, or casting magic. They give you new weapons, armor, or spells."

"This game's easy," Katie said, pulling her DragonSword out of the package. The purple spheres above our heads returned to full size and then disappeared.

We walked confidently into the commoners' village. A little girl pointed at Katie and screamed, "The Princess of the West!" The rest of the villagers fell to their knees and looked at the ground.

Suddenly black clouds covered the sun. A rectangle tumbled through the sky until it crashed nearby, sending a flume of dirt into the air. Giant words on the rectangle read "THIS PROGRAM HAS PERFORMED AN ILLEGAL OPERATION AND WILL BE SHUT DOWN." Two icons labeled "OK" and "CLOSE" sat underneath.

"Which one do I press?" Katie asked, staring at the icons as large hail fell from the clouds.

I hit the "CLOSE" button, which transformed Katie and me back into humans. My bedroom appeared, and we crash-landed on my pile of stuffed animals. That's when I noticed two things: "ERROR—NOT ENOUGH MEMORY" was flashing on my computer screen, and we still had all of our *DragonSteel* equipment and clothes!

"This can't be happening, this can't be happening," Katie said in a frenzy. She quickly removed the sash from her forehead and stuck it in her backpack. "My mom better not notice these baggy pants."

"Oh, no! Aidan *said* we wouldn't be able to stop playing," I remembered, scrambling over to my dresser. I put on pants under my robe.

"But we're *not* playing the game now, so why do we still have these virtual clothes?" Katie asked, bewildered.

"I don't get how a game can change the real world," I said, as I jammed the robe into the bottom drawer.

"Why can't you and I do normal things like other people?" Katie complained, putting the DragonSword in her backpack. "Like watch TV or something."

After Katie went home, I curled up on my pile of stuffed animals. I could hardly believe we had played the computer game. Maybe I had napped and dreamed it all? But the robe, the spell book— they were *real*. It had to be true! I decided to choose a cool warrior like Ignatia next time we played the game.

I opened my spell book. Big red X's crossed out the spells *Divide and Conquer* and *Divine Intelligence* on the first two pages. Only one spell remained: *Reveal Truth*. The fancy illustration showed a cartoon boy pointing at a hideous winged lizard labeled "Dark Minion." A bubble came out of the minion's mouth with the words "I have only a few hitpoints and low intelligence, but I possess the power to travel between dimensions." The old-fashioned writing under the picture read "Ye shall point and ye shall know all that is hidden from thine eyes."

"This could come in handy," I said, excited at the possibilities.

THE COMPUTER GAME BRINGS TROUBLE

On Monday I brought my spell book to school because I had a big English test. As usual, I hadn't paid attention in class. Mom and Dad claim that I fail things because I don't try, but they don't know what it's like to be me—I just can't concentrate. They said I would lose the computer if I failed anything else, so I came up with a plan.

"OK, clear your desks," Mr. O said, passing out the tests. Before putting my books away, I pressed my index finger against *Reveal Truth* in my spell book. Then I cleared my desk, careful not to touch anything with my glowing finger.

After Mr. O gave me my test, I waited until he walked away, and then I pointed at the answer sheet. At once all the answers filled in, just like I'd hoped! Katie looked at me with disapproval.

Suddenly a loud dinging broke the silence, and the giant bubble letters "PowerUp Bonus!" flew

43

around the classroom. A poof of white smoke briefly enveloped Katie and me, transforming her clothes into a full suit of leather armor and mine into a bright yellow robe. A wooden staff with an intricately carved dragon's head appeared in my hand. The wooden dragon breathed fire, sizzling my test into black bits.

"Fire drill!" Mr. O announced as the dinging continued. The class lined up to leave the room.

"I'm gonna get grounded *again*," I whined, certain that Mars would be colonized by the time my punishment for this ended.

I tried to explain everything later in the principal's office.

"What do you mean, you *powered up*?" Principal

Brumby said, pacing back and forth behind his desk. He soon became tired and plopped into his chair.

"Well, uh, I got a fire-breathing dragon staff as a bonus for casting spells in this game we're—"

"Sir," Katie interrupted, "we just made a mistake. Joe and I thought today was Halloween. That's why we're dressed so funny."

"Halloween isn't until the middle of next week," the principal informed us. "Very well, I'm suspending both of you until then. Your parents are on their way with a change of clothes, and I'm confiscating all these unusual belongings." Brumby put the spell book and DragonStaff in a trunk and locked it.

Later that day I sat on the stairs and listened to Mom and Dad argue about how to punish me. I vowed to quit fantasy games forever if they would just stop spazzing over me. I even considered staring at ancient rocks for fun, just to make my parents happy.

"He set off the fire alarm in school?" Dad screamed, pacing back and forth. "Is this what he does when we're working on the Acropolis—wear women's underwear and dresses and set the school on fire?"

"For the last time, it wasn't a dress, it was a robe!" Mom hollered. "Just calm down. Remember, there's always that boarding school idea we discussed."

I slammed my door and threw myself onto my pile of stuffed animals.

"I saw everything," Snuffles said to me in a high-pitched voice. "You have to quit that computer game. It's making you look bad."

"Without you, we would all be in the garbage dump," Koala Bear 3 said.

I stood up, grabbed the *DragonSteel* CD, and plopped back onto my bear pile.

"How can I quit a game I'm not even running right now?" I said in bewilderment, staring at my reflection in the shiny CD. I puzzled over this all evening until I sank deeper into my bear pile and fell asleep.

Aidan spoke to me in my dream later that night. "You can't quit. The Great Prophecy says that once the Earthlings have begun the quest, the amulet piece hidden in your world will magically appear. You *must* find it—but beware, the Emperor of the West will sense the strong magic, and he'll send a dark minion to get the missing piece first. He stubbornly believes he can defy the prophecy and reunite the amulet himself."

I woke up sweating in the middle of the night.

"It's just a game," I told Snuffles, hugging him tightly. "It can't be real."

I ENCOUNTER EVIL AT THE SUPERMARKET

The next day Mom stayed home so she could keep an eye on me. I even had to go to the grocery store with her—yuck!

"I promise, no more fantasy stuff," I told her in the car.

"You have a big hole to dig out of, young man," Mom said. "You get in trouble in Mr. O's class almost every day, and this time it's serious. Not to mention you're failing three subjects. Why can't you just be like other kids and behave?"

"But I'm not the only one who goofs off," I argued. "Brian reads comic books in class all the time, and he never gets in trouble."

"You are not Brian," Mom said angrily. "Anyway, I don't care what anybody else is doing. Your father and I are very tense right now because the Acropolis project has to be completed in two weeks. Our supervisor is flying in from Greece to inspect it, and

47

she's bringing some important people. The Acropolis *must* look exactly as it did in the fifth century B.C. I don't have time to watch you every second."

"Are you really going to send me to boarding school?" I asked nervously.

"You shouldn't be eavesdropping on our conversations," she answered coldly.

In the supermarket, Mom read from her grocery list, and I ran to get everything. We made a pretty good team. She even smiled once when I picked out the fat-free Fig Newtons instead of the regular kind that I normally get.

"We need two boxes of granola cereal, the kind with raisins and dates," Mom directed.

In the cereal aisle a small girl wearing a pink bonnet hopped up and down in front of the Cheerios. She tried to reach a box on a high shelf, saying, "O's, O's" over and over again. That's when I noticed a strange cereal mixed in with the ordinary boxes—a shiny silver box labeled "Dragon-Steel O's." A picture of the English Golem sat on the front of the box, and a cartoon bubble coming out of his mouth contained the words "Now made from 100% sugar! Dat's Salubrious!"

"Gimme box, gimme box," the girl said, hopping up and down.

"OK, I'll get it for you," I told her, reaching for

the shiny box. I was about to hand it over when I noticed the words "Free inside this cereal—the DragonSteel Amulet Base!" A picture of the DragonSteel Amulet lacking the four gems sat in a bright blue circle. Aidan's mysterious prophecy had come true!

"Mom, we gotta get this cereal," I said, running up to her with the DragonSteel box.

"That cereal is all sugar," Mom said, pushing it away. "I asked you to get granola." The young girl wandered up to Mom and bawled her eyes out while reaching for the box.

"But Mom, I need this cereal to fight the forces of evil!" I told her.

"You said that about a box of double fudge ice cream last time," Mom said, snatching the box from me and handing it to the girl.

"Tank you," the girl said in a sweet voice. She turned to me and giggled, and then all the skin above her neck suddenly fell off, revealing a cartoon lizard face. She hissed at me and extended a long tongue in my direction.

"She's a dark minion!" I announced, chasing the creature down the aisle while Mom looked on in horror. I tackled the minion, causing it to drop the box.

"Meddle no further in the affairs of our world,"

the minion said in a deep voice. The rest of the little girl's exterior fell off. Giant wings sprouted on both sides of the minion's body, and a mysterious force sent me flying down the aisle. I landed near the farina.

"Mom, duck!" I yelled, grabbing a tin of farina off the shelf. I hurled the tin at the minion as it climbed the shelves.

I scored a direct hit, and the creature crashed to the floor with a gooey, crunching noise. Yellow liquid oozed from its carcass, eating a hole through the tiles.

"I told you, I need this cereal," I reminded Mom, who stood in shock next to our wagon. I pushed her and the wagon toward the checkout aisles. "Trust me, Mom."

"Cleanup in aisle nine," a voice blared over the loudspeaker. "Cleanup in aisle nine."

Later, I held the DragonSteel Amulet Base and sat in my usual place at the top of the stairs. The intricately carved dragon's head contained four empty slots for the enchanted stones, surrounded by incomprehensible writing. As Mom and Dad argued down in the kitchen, the object vibrated in my hand. Strange. My legs started itching terribly, and then the vibrating stopped.

"He's beating up little girls now?" Dad hollered, slamming the refrigerator door shut.

"I'm not entirely sure what happened," Mom admitted. "I was in a daze. I think all that fantasy talk is starting to take its toll."

"Tomorrow all his fantasy stuff is going in the garbage," Dad said. "The computer games, the cards, the posters—everything."

I ran into my room and called Katie. "Come over *now*," I ordered.

"I can't," she said. "I'm being punished."

"Sneak out and climb up the tree outside my window. I don't know what's going on, but it's bad."

I DUEL A THIEF

Later that day, I showed Katie the steel dragon's head and explained everything that had happened at the supermarket. We both agreed to run the *DragonSteel* CD again and try to quit this messed-up game, no matter how cool it once seemed. It was just too dangerous.

"You should've seen the look on my mom's face when I defeated the minion," I said, putting the Amulet Base in Katie's backpack.

"This is the craziest, spookiest thing we've ever gotten into," Katie responded as she retrieved her DragonSword and strapped on her pack. I inserted the CD labeled "I. SCHLEPP" into my computer and booted it up. At once Katie and I transformed back into cartoons and appeared in Komondor.

A deserted heap of rubble sat in place of the commoners' village. Aidan stood next to the ruins and tapped his purple foot impatiently. Then he waved

his hand, restoring our game clothes.

"We want to quit," I told Aidan, adjusting my yellow robe.

"You can't quit until the DragonSteel Amulet is complete," Aidan said. "Now you *must* finish the quest by finding all four enchanted gems and inserting them into the Amulet Base."

"Why can't we quit?"

"Because you're the *Chosen Ones*, duh," Aidan answered.

"What do you mean we're the Chosen Ones? Find different Chosen Ones," I insisted. "Katie and I are getting in big trouble because of all this."

"All the other kids who won the *DragonSteel* card game bought the Everything Box from my store so they could make wishes," Aidan began. "But you guys picked the computer game, so you're the Chosen Ones. No take-backs or do-overs—that's what the Great Prophecy says. If you don't like it you can complain to Syzygy, Keeper of the Fates, who lives in the Forbidden Cwm in the Peaks of Doom."

"Fine, we will," I said stubbornly, "but I want a new character first. This magician's lame, and he has a dorky robe."

"I told you to wait for a cool warrior," Aidan said, handing me a new spell book and DragonStaff. "You can't start over. I need rare ingredients to cast those spells, and the characters you have now will last long enough to finish the quest."

"What spells?" I asked.

"Uh, I'll explain everything later—you're wasting time. The Emperor of the West is out searching for the Amulet Base that you found. Now keep up the good work and go steal the Sapphire DragonFlame from his castle while he's away. Don't wake the crystalline serpent, though." Aidan waved his hands and disappeared.

"I don't like this," Katie said nervously. "That emperor might hurt us. And what happens if we lose the game?"

"Let's just finish the quest quickly and get out of here."

With no other choice, Katie and I followed the path north into a dark forest. As we walked, tiny pink squirrels covered with loopy Velcro fur jumped from vines and attached themselves to latchy Velcro trees. The forest was loud because of the ripping sounds of Velcro coming undone.

Near nightfall we realized that all of our equipment was missing!

"Did we drop everything?" Katie asked anxiously, looking at the path behind her.

"I would have noticed if you dropped your backpack and sword," I said, eyeing the chattering creatures above us suspiciously.

Suddenly a masked boy wearing black clothing jumped in front of us. His giant cartoon eyes peeked through the mask, and he had an immense shock of black hair.

"Who's that I see?" he said, hopping onto a nearby rock and dramatically scanning the horizon. "Could it be? Why, yes, it *is*!" He jumped off the rock and got down on one knee before Katie, extending an arm to the ground. "It's the beautiful Princess Ignatia! At your service, ma'am."

"Who are you?" Katie asked.

The boy hopped onto the rock again and put his arms akimbo, looking heroically off into the distance. "Wherever jewels are found, *I'll* be near. Wherever wallets hide, *I'll* be there. Wherever thievery thrives, *I'll* be causing it. My name is ... Michael Bottompockets!" He leaped in front of Katie, opening an ancient-looking bag. "What do we have for the princess today? A magical backpack containing a metal dragon's head? A spell book with lame magician spells? A DragonStaff and Drag-onSword?" He pulled all our stuff out of his bag.

"Hey, you stole our stuff!" I said.

"Not everything, JuJu," Michael sneered, hop-ping in front of me. "I let you keep that fashionable yellow robe you're wearing."

"Hey, that's not fair, I *wanted* to be a warrior. I didn't know you couldn't restart the game."

"What game?" Michael asked with a puzzled look.

"You know, this whole neat-looking 3D world," I answered, glancing around.

"Oh, that," Michael said. "The Emperor of the West has agreed not to arrest all the thieves as long as we keep our forest clean." He kneeled in front of Katie again and said, "I envy you, Princess, because you have the one thing I can never steal—true beauty."

"Oh, stop with the mush!" I demanded. "She's *my* girlfriend!"

"Looks like Magic Boy wants to duel," Michael said, tossing me my spell book and staff. "*Com-mence Duel!*" After a flash of light, two purple spheres hovered over us.

Angry, I opened my spell book. I had three new spells: *Limb Freeze, Make Friendly,* and *Summon Nana.*

"Take this, thief!" I said, casting *Limb Freeze*. Michael's arms and legs became frozen. I comboed that with *Summon Nana*, which I hoped would conjure a powerful beast. Instead, a gray-haired woman wearing hair curlers appeared next to Michael.

"Michael, did you steal the cookies from the cookie jar?" the woman said, shaking a finger at Michael.

"I didn't steal the cookies from the cookie jar," Michael said.

"Then *who* stole the cookies from the cookie jar?" the woman sang.

"JuJu stole the cookies from the cookie jar," Michael sang, still unable to move his arms and legs.

"JuJu, did *you* steal the cookies from the cookie jar?" she sang, walking toward me.

"Ha! Everybody knows how to avoid Nana," Michael said. "That's a baby spell."

I sent Nana back over to Michael, and then I cast *Make Friendly* on her. Suddenly Nana smiled and squeezed Michael's cheek, saying, "Land sakes, how you've grown, Michael!" Pretty soon she had both cheeks in a tight grip, and the purple sphere over Michael's head shrank halfway. Unfortunately, Nana soon disappeared in a puff of smoke, and my freeze spell wore off.

"Pretty good, you knocked off a lot of hitpoints," Michael said, pulling a black net surrounded by spikes out of his bag. "But not good enough." He waved the net in the air, creating a whizzing noise. "Prepare to lose!"

"You better not hurt Joe with that," Katie warned, hopping off the rock where she had been sitting.

Disappointed, Michael put the net back in his black bag. "As you wish, Princess," he said solemnly, bowing to her. "Duel completed." The purple spheres vanished.

Rescued by my girlfriend. Ugh!

"Be nice to Joe. Uh, I mean JuJu. We have to get moving," Katie said impatiently. "We're supposed to go to the castle, and it's already nighttime. We're on a quest to complete the DragonSteel Amulet."

"Be careful, Princess, your father is nearby," Michael said. "He recently ransacked the commoners' village because you were spotted there."

"But my father is a plumber," Katie declared, looking puzzled.

"Uh, OK, whatever you say, Princess," Michael said. "Follow me. I can take you as far as the Bridge of the Maladroit Guardians."

Michael lit a torch and led us through the forest. The path skirted steep cliffs, which looked like bottomless pits in the darkness. We crossed a creaky overpass made from rotting wood and tattered ropes. Strange creatures clucked from hidden places as we journeyed farther into the night. Eventually the forest ended beside a deep chasm. In the distance a creepy castle stood on a shadowy crag, illuminated now and then by lightning bolts.

"Just follow this path to get to your home, Princess—the Western Kingdom," Michael said, pointing at a narrow strip of rock that led to a torch-lit bridge. "I have to go now. If I stay away from home too long my dad starts stealing my stuff. Until we meet again, Princess." Michael bowed and then disappeared into the night.

Katie and I timidly took a few steps onto the strip of rock, causing loose pieces of stone to tumble into the chasm. The lightning revealed crashing waves far down at the bottom. I held Katie's hand so that I wouldn't lose my balance.

"He's a nice guy," Katie said, tiptoeing toward the bridge.

"Not as nice as me," I said. "Right?"

WE EXPLORE A CREEPY CASTLE

A small yellow dwarf and a big green troll guarded the wooden bridge. We crouched beyond the torchlight and listened to them talk.

"But Bantam, Guano does clean self," the troll said in a deep voice, scratching a wart on his forehead. "Guano washed self last week."

"You fell off the bridge, Guano," the dwarf said quickly in a high-pitched tone. "That doesn't count. Face it, you're a smelly troll with no personal hygiene. No wonder nobody ever wants to cross this bridge!"

"Bantam not right. Guano take good care of teeth so Guano can eats dwarfies."

"Your teeth are black and crusty!" Bantam said, jumping in the air. "And they're all crooked!"

"But there no pieces of dwarfy stuck between teeth," Guano said, smiling widely at Bantam to show off. "Guano's dentist show Guano funny trick to keep teeth clean, but Guano forget what trick called."

"It's irritating how you can so flippantly talk about eating dwarves all the time," Bantam said, kicking Guano's leg. "I'm putting in for a transfer to another bridge."

"Guano would miss Bantam," the troll said, "and how Guano guard whole bridge by self?"

"How many times have I told you, *use personal pronouns!*" Bantam squeaked. "*I* would miss *you*."

"Is nice that Bantam would miss Guano. Guano now have warm feeling inside."

Bantam began banging his head against the side of the bridge. It made me giggle.

"Guano, did you hear that noise?" Bantam asked, running to the edge of the bridge. "There, in the darkness. Somebody wants to cross the bridge!"

"Guano's turn to say phrase," Guano said, clomping to the edge.

"No," Bantam argued. "You always mess it up."

"Bantam say phrase last time."

"Fine, I don't care who says it," Bantam declared, crossing his arms.

Katie and I walked cautiously toward the bridge. When we came into the light, the troll cleared his throat, put a large, wart-ridden hand out to us, and said, *"None shall floss!"*

"Ooohh!" Bantam screeched. "See, you messed it up! It's *cross,* not *floss*! You're a big stupid troll that can't do anything right!"

"At least Guano remember what teeth-cleaning trick called," Guano said.

"Who cares? You'll forget it tomorrow because you're so *dumb*!"

"Me bash *you* now," Guano said angrily, stomping toward Bantam with a clenched fist. "How Bantam like dem pronouns?"

Bantam ducked through Guano's legs and ran off the bridge toward the Thieves' Forest, saying, "You'll never catch me, you'll never catch me."

Katie pulled me across the bridge while Guano lumbered after the speedy dwarf. We followed a narrow winding trail toward the castle. When we neared the entrance, the bubble words "PowerUp Bonus!" flew around in the air until they were struck by lightning and fell apart. As thunder crackled above the castle, Katie's armor changed from leather to copper and a bunch of polka dots appeared on my yellow robe. I hoped my new spells weren't as dorky as my clothes.

"If Princess Ignatia once lived in this castle, then they should let us in," Katie said, clanking the iron knockers on the huge wooden door.

"I don't know—Aidan and Michael Bottompockets made it sound like the Emperor of the West is pretty upset at you," I pointed out.

A few minutes later the door creaked open, and we crept into the gloomy castle. Giant tapestries depicting ancient battles hung on the wall. Enormous suits of steel armor stood around us, holding scary weapons. Katie and I held on to each other as footsteps scurried nearby.

"I must be dreaming," a girl said, wandering out of the darkness and giving Katie a hug. "How I've missed you, Princess!" The girl had pointy purple hair with one unusually large spike coming out of it, and she held an enormous broom.

"Who are you?" Katie asked.

"It's Eryn, the scullery maid! Have you forgotten me after all your exciting adventures? I see you've found a boyfriend."

"Um, can you help us find the Sapphire DragonFlame?" I asked nervously, hoping the girl wouldn't realize that Katie was only pretending to be Princess Ignatia. "We're in a hurry."

"Princess, you don't want to get mixed up in all of that. Your father will get even angrier. He's already upset that you refuse to marry Prince Kivin."

"Please, Eryn, we have to finish the DragonSteel Amulet quest," Katie pleaded. "It's the only way to quit the game and, uh, get back to normal."

"The emperor *did* say he

wants you stop playing games and accept your responsibilities as a princess," Eryn returned. "OK, follow me."

Eryn led us deep into the interior of the castle—through secret doors, down ancient cobwebby steps, across moss-covered stone bridges. Eventually we entered a huge underground cavern lit by jewels jutting from the walls. A glowing sphere containing the Sapphire DragonFlame floated in the center of the room. A sparkling serpent slept peacefully underneath. Its body wrapped around the cavern three times.

"You'll never beat the serpent by yourself," Eryn whispered. "It's too powerful. But I'll show you a secret that most people don't know about." She tapped a rock on the wall, and a nearby panel flipped open. Inside, a glass dome contained fluffy slippers shaped like sheep. A sign read "Break Glass to Acquire Magic No-Disturb Slippers."

"It's a trick," Eryn whispered, pushing me away from the dome just as I reached forward to follow the sign's instructions. "The serpent always wakes up when you break the glass. You have to get this first." She opened another secret compartment, which contained a plastic bag labeled "Magic No-Noise Hammer."

"Hurry, hurry!" Eryn said as I hammered the

glass and put on the slippers. "Don't waste even a second."

I walked nervously down a stone staircase and crept over the sleeping serpent. Before long, I stood next to the glowing sphere and admired the Sapphire DragonFlame within. The sparkling breath of fire soon made my eyes burn, and I had to look away.

My hand passed effortlessly through the transparent sphere, and a warm feeling overcame me when I gripped the orange jewel. Odd. My nose twitched, and I began whimpering. Confused, I quickly placed the DragonFlame in my pocket and walked toward the entrance of the vault, where Eryn and Katie waved me on. As I walked over the serpent this time, my slippers said, "Baaa, baaa." The noise echoed around the cavern.

"Who daresss disssturb the crysssstalline sssserpent!" a deep voice said. The serpent's coils stacked together, and a giant purple sphere appeared in the air.

"Hurry, Joe!" Katie cried, pulling out her DragonSword. My heart raced as I sprinted for the door. Before I reached the stone steps, a shadow fell over me. The serpent grabbed me in its mouth and lifted me into the air.

"Help!" I hollered, banging my DragonStaff against the serpent's jaw.

"Let him go, you monster!" Katie cried, leaping down the stairs. She swiped her DragonSword over a bar code on the creature's tail, creating a virtual serpent that extended to the roof of the cavern. When she mashed some buttons on the handle all at once, the hologram began to hiss, lunge, and bite.

The real serpent imprisoned me in the center of its coiled body and focused on Katie. I quickly pulled the spell book out of my robe and looked at my three new spells: *Gales of Laughter, Levitate,* and *Imitate.*

"Hang on!" I shouted, casting *Levitate* on myself. Immediately I blew up like a balloon and floated out of control toward the ceiling. "I'm gonna put a spell on the serpent—watch out!" I pressed my finger on *Gales of Laughter,* but just as I pointed at the serpent my inflated body popped on a sharp stalactite. The outflow of air sent me flying all over the cavern. I heard Katie laughing down below. I had accidentally cast the spell on her!

"Joe, you popped!" she said, laughing uncontrollably. The DragonSword slipped to the ground and rolled toward the serpent. Katie fell on her back and said "Popped!" in a high-pitched giggle.

"Whoooaaahh!" I cried as I dizzily zoomed all over the cavern. A perfect opportunity to save my girlfriend, and I blew it!

"What is the meaning of this!" a booming voice said. A hooded figure wearing a giant cape stood by the entrance to the chamber. Six growling minions surrounded him. At once the serpent slithered back under the glowing sphere and went to sleep.

"Emperor!" Eryn cried, dropping to her knees.

"Do my eyes deceive me?" the emperor asked, walking over to Katie. He pulled back his hood, revealing a hideous face and a bar code on his forehead. "My daughter has returned at last!"

"You're ugly!" Katie said, emitting deep belly laughs and pointing at the emperor's face. At that moment my spells wore off, and I fell onto the emperor, knocking him to the ground.

"What is that wretched JuJu doing here?" the emperor roared. Three minions hopped over and grabbed me while the rest of them helped the emperor to his feet. "Ignatia, you know very well that I've planned a marriage between you and Prince Kivin of the Eastern Kingdom. His family possesses the Red DragonEye!" The emperor snapped a finger, and a minion searched Katie's backpack and my robe.

"Master, look at these wonderful trinkets," the minion said in a deep voice, running over to the emperor with the Amulet Base and the Dragon-Flame.

"Those aren't trinkets, you idiot!" the emperor said, snatching them. "The long-lost Amulet Base! The DragonFlame!" He quickly snapped the orange jewel into the corresponding slot on the base. A jet of fire erupted from the jewel momentarily. "After the marriage alliance with the Eastern Kingdom, the Red DragonEye will also be mine, leaving only two sacred pieces of the amulet to be found. Never have I been so close to ultimate power! And that foolish prophecy said only Earthlings could do it! When I reunite all five pieces of the DragonSteel Amulet, I will transform into the most divine creature in the universe! At long last Komondor will be united under one supreme ruler again—*me*! When that day comes, the first thing I shall do is destroy Earth. No longer will that filthy planet meddle in Komondor's affairs!" His booming voice loosened rocks from the ceiling, which hit the ground and shattered.

"You're not my father!" Katie shrieked, stepping forward boldly. "And I will never marry against my wishes!"

"We shall soon see who's in control here," the emperor challenged. "Minions! Lock my daughter in her room! And take the magician and that backstabbing scullery maid and throw them in the Infernal Dungeon. If Ignatia does not agree to marry Prince Kivin by the next full moon, the dungeon shall be filled with lava!"

At once the minions grabbed me and Eryn and bounded down a hallway, drooling and grunting. We traveled through a complicated maze of secret doors, ladders, and moving platforms until we arrived at a dungeon deep within the bowels of Komondor.

"Enjoy your stay," a minion said in a guttural tone.

"You shall find it most accommodating," another added. "I know the toxic rats do."

The minions opened a hatch and threw Eryn and me into the pit. As we tumbled through the blackness, my stomach felt queasy, the way it does when you fall in a dream. Suddenly the room became very bright, and I landed on my dad! He held my computer's power cord in his hand. Moments later Katie fell on top of both of us.

"Who are you?" Dad asked nervously as we all scrambled to our feet.

I looked down at myself. My body looked bright and colorful, and my polka-dotted yellow robe glowed with its own energy. Katie and I stared at each other in shock.

We were still cartoons.

CARTOONS IN THE REAL WORLD

"Dad, it's me," I said frantically. "And that's Katie. We transformed into cartoon characters from a computer game."

"What? Is this some sort of prank?" Dad asked, eyeing my tower of hair curiously. "Change back this instant before your mother sees you!"

"I have to go home," Katie said in a panic, grabbing her DragonSword. "My parents are probably looking for me." She opened the window and jumped onto the oak tree with unusual agility.

"Fred, I just asked you to get him back in bed," Mom said, walking into the room with her nightgown on.

"Something's very wrong, honey," Dad said tremulously, rubbing his eyes.

"I know," Mom agreed, guiding me over to my bed. "Joe, you've been grounded, you're suspended from school, and you're still up at midnight! When are we going to get through to you?"

"But Mom, I'm a Japanimation," I whined. She squinted. I could tell she wasn't wearing her contact lenses.

"You're not Japanese," Mom said, tucking me under the covers. "It must've been a dream."

When Mom shut off the light, my eyes lit up the room like a night-light. Dad looked bewildered.

When I was still a cartoon the next day, my parents freaked out and called in Dad's friend Dr. Zaretsky.

He snapped pictures, took blood samples, and told me to take two Tylenol every six hours. Meanwhile, Dad took all the fantasy stuff out of my room, leaving only my pile of bears. Then Mom and Dad brought chairs next to my bed and stared at me all day.

"I'm sorry I've caused so much trouble lately," I said, inching toward Mom. "Katie and I are in a big mess that we can't get out of. *Please* don't send me to boarding school."

"Don't worry, honey," Mom said, leaning over and hugging me tightly. "We're not going to send you anywhere, we promise." I cried so hard that a steady stream of tears flew out of my eyes, but they disappeared in mid-air.

"Dr. Zaretsky will get to the bottom of this," Dad said.

"It'll all be fine, Joe," Mom reassured me hesitantly, patting my shoulder. "You're at that awkward age. It's probably just a hormonal thing." She didn't sound like she believed her own words. I had to figure out a way to get back to Komondor *fast*.

"You should've seen *me* when I was twelve," Dad added.

"How's the Acropolis going?" I asked, trying to change the subject.

"The grand opening is in a couple of weeks," Dad said. "After three years of hard work, the buildings look exactly as they did in the fifth century B.C."

"The most challenging was the Propylaea—the elaborate archway," Mom said. "Surprisingly, the hard part about reconstructing that building was getting the workers to distinguish between the Ionic and Doric columns—they mixed them up originally, setting back our building schedule by ..."

I tried to figure out a plan while Mom droned on. Luckily, being a mutant cartoon wasn't painful at all.

The next day Dr. Zaretsky called to say that my DNA contained a triple helix instead of a double one, which might explain my colorful appearance. He mailed my blood sample to the Centers for Disease Control in Atlanta, Georgia.

"They're specialists," Mom said. "They can cure anything."

I wasn't so sure, unless they were experts on super-advanced computer games too. Or maybe I just had the worst computer virus ever.

"Dr. Zaretsky said you're not contagious," Dad added. "*That's* good news, anyway."

Mom and Dad stayed home with me all week. They defended me when Katie's dad stormed into our house and accused me of being a juvenile delinquent. After a while, they even calmed down about my freakishness and said I could go to school next week after my suspension ended. I called Katie every day, but her parents hung up on me. I finally got through to her over the weekend.

"Joe, I'm still a mutant," Katie cried over the phone. "What's happening to us?"

"Come over tonight after everybody's asleep," I instructed. "We have to finish the quest to be free of the game, just like Aidan warned."

"I can't, my dad's totally going bonkers," Katie returned, sobbing. "He's guarding my door now. I described Komondor to him, but he didn't believe me. He said a Komondor is a big fluffy dog, and his friend *has* one."

"Your dad doesn't know much about fantasy games," I observed.

"No, he likes cribbage."

"Is that a vegetable?"

"You and your vegetables!" Katie laughed. "I miss you, Joe. I gotta go. Don't run the game without me or you'll be drowned in lava."

CAPTURED!

Katie and I decided to go to school on Wednesday. Sitting around the house was way too boring, and we didn't want to miss the chance to impress all the kids. Anyway, it was Halloween, so everybody at the bus stop was dressed up.

"Wow, awesome costume, Katie," Nikki said. "You look just like Ignatia from *DragonSteel!*"

"I'll give you my birthday presents for a whole year if you make me look like an anime warrior," Max offered.

Pretty soon everybody was crowding around Katie. Nobody wanted to see me in my dorky polka-dotted yellow robe, not even the first-graders. I was so mad at myself for not choosing a cool warrior—I could have been a hero to the kids, just like I always imagined.

Katie pressed a button on her sword, and a computerized voice said, "Activating DragonSword demonstration program now." A harmless holo-gram of a dragon flew out the end of her sword handle, and Katie swung it around.

"That's the coolest thing *ever*," Eric said.

"Magic is cooler," I insisted, opening my spell book. I put my finger on the spell *Imitate* and then pointed at Katie. At once I turned into Ignatia. I ran around the pack of kids shouting, "Look, I can be a dumb warrior too!" Pretending to fight a mon-ster, I dove onto the ground and desperately swung my DragonSword. After a minute I changed back into JuJu. Nobody had noticed, and I felt like an even bigger dork.

Suddenly a black helicopter landed in the middle of the street, nearly hitting some electrical wires with its blades. A man and a woman wearing hi-tech uniforms jumped out and ran toward the bus stop. Goosebumps covered my whole body when I realized they were heading directly for me!

"Run!" I shouted as a burst of strength swept through me. Katie and I sprinted onto a side street, but two white vans converged in front of us, blocking our escape. The van doors slid open, and three people wearing space suits walked toward us like zombies. I hoped that this was another bad daydream.

"Come with us, please," the uniformed woman

said, taking our hands and pulling us toward the helicopter. "It's in the interest of national security."

The crowd of costumed kids watched as the helicopter carried Katie and me into the air. Barney the Dinosaur waved.

"Don't try anything funny," the uniformed man said, showing me a shiny badge. "FBI. I'm Agent Brasch, and this is Agent Alderman."

"Some people in Atlanta want to meet you," Agent Alderman said, looking at me anxiously.

The helicopter flew over Mom and Dad's Acropolis, which majestically overlooked the bay. I held Katie's hand during the whole ride, imagining what Mom and Dad would say when they found out that I was nabbed by the FBI. It all seemed hopeless now. Unless we got back to Komondor and finished the quest, we'd be stuck as cartoons forever, trapped in some secret government lab used for gross experiments. I wanted to cry, but I held it in so Katie wouldn't think I was a wimp.

The building we landed on looked like something from ancient Greece, with big white columns and fancy carvings. The agents brought Katie and me into a high-security FBI office and sat us at a slick black table.

"Let's get right down to business," Agent Alderman said, placing a newspaper clipping on

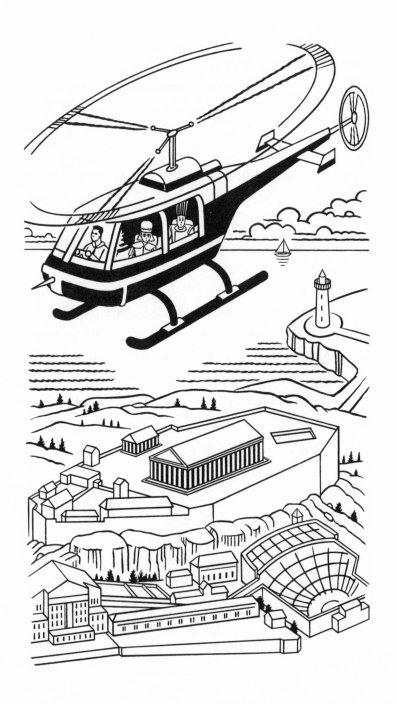

the table. "What can you tell us about this article?"

CLAUDIA'S COMFORTS EMPLOYEES CLAIM UFO ABDUCTION

Monday, October 22.

At 6:03 P.M. last Friday, Claudia's Comforts, a popular women's underwear store in Long Island's Smithhaven Mall, vanished. Witnesses claim that a glowing store called Aidan's Curiosities appeared in its place. When curious customers tried to enter this mysterious new store, an invisible forcefield kept them out. Yet two children, a boy and a girl, were seen casually entering and exiting the store before everything changed back to normal.

What happened to the Claudia's Comforts employees during this time? They claim that they were abducted by aliens. They say that the mall outside the store vanished and was replaced by a colorful forest containing cartoonlike creatures with unusually large eyes and substantial quantities of hair. They remained in that world for approximately ten minutes. Then the mall reappeared, and everything returned to normal. Paranormal

*researchers, scientists, and the FBI are cur-
rently investigating. If you have any information regarding this strange occurrence,
please contact your local police department
immediately.*

"How many more of you are there?" Agent
Brasch asked, slamming his hand on the table.

"We're not aliens!" Katie insisted, pushing the
article away. "I want a lawyer."

"I wanna call home," I said stubbornly, determined not to tell them anything about the computer game. "My parents are probably spazzing by
now."

"Where's *home?*" Agent Brasch sneered. "Earth?
Or the planet *Gookimunkus?*"

"What my partner means is that we can't let you
talk to anyone until doctors from the Centers for
Disease Control have examined you," Agent
Alderman said, frowning at Agent Brasch. "They
were very alarmed by your blood samples. You'll
be quarantined here until further notice."

WE ATTEMPT TWO DARING ESCAPES

FORM 1040—UFO

Place an "X" in the appropriate boxes.
Mark all that apply.

I have the following special powers:
- ☐ I can read minds
- ☐ I can travel through time
- ☐ I can warp to distant parts of the universe
- ☐ I can fly
- ☐ I have x-ray vision
- ☒ Other (specify) _I can blow bubbles with my tongue_

I work for the following people or organizations:
- ☐ A mad scientist
- ☐ An alien government
- ☐ An evil sorcerer

☒ Other (specify) _The FBI_

I plan to use my powers:
☐ For good
☐ For evil
☒ Other (specify) _To win the annual Alaskan bubble-blowing contest_

"You're just going to make it harder for yourself if you don't cooperate," Agent Brasch said, pulling the form away from me. He looked hopelessly at Agent Alderman.

"Maybe it'll help if they eat something," Agent Alderman said. "Do you two want dinner?"

"Maybe cartoon aliens don't need food," Agent Brasch said with his usual sneer.

"Fine, I'll eat, but no dead animals," I said, crossing my arms.

Later that evening they locked Katie and me in adjacent cells. I was still trying to act brave for Katie even though I was scared. What if we couldn't finish the quest? We'd never get out of this game. We talked through most of the night.

"I wonder if this _is_ a game," Katie said. "It's too real."

"What else could it be?" I asked.

"I don't know, but if it's not a game, then we

won't be able to start over if we lose, or—"

"Don't say that," I interrupted. "It's just virtual reality. It's *supposed* to seem real."

"But how come we've been playing it without the CD?"

"I don't know," I answered. "I have some questions for—"

Suddenly Aidan appeared in my cell. "You two stink at being the Chosen Ones," he said in disgust.

"Aidan, why are we still cartoons?" I asked frantically. "How come the game won't let us stop playing?"

"I warned you," Aidan said, shaking his index finger at me. "Uh, I'll explain later. The security guard's gonna come by any second, so you have to get back in the game right now. Follow me."

He waved a hand, and the doors to our cells opened automatically. When we stepped into the hallway, all the lights in the building suddenly came on and a siren blared.

"Stop right there!" a guard ordered, running toward us. I froze in shock.

"Hurry!" Aidan commanded. Katie pulled me into a stairwell, and the three of us ran to the next floor. When Aidan waved his arms, all the office doors flew open and the computers turned on.

Aidan placed the CD labeled "I. SCHLEPP" into

a computer just as the guard burst out of the stairwell. I abruptly found myself in a gloomy cartoon
dungeon filled with glowing green rats. Aidan
stood next to me, adjusting his bright yellow shirt
sleeve. For a brief moment I thought I saw a bar
code on his upper arm.

"There's going to be a full moon tonight," he said.
"The emperor plans to fill this dungeon with lava
soon. The prophecy forbids me from rescuing the
Chosen Ones anywhere in Komondor, so you'd better
escape fast." He waved his hand and disappeared.

"But Aidan, wait!" I cried, wondering when he
would explain everything to me. I looked around at
the gloom. Strange. I had escaped, only to be

trapped again. And where was Katie?

Eryn was there, though. "Where were you?" she asked, running over to me and giving me a hug. "It's so lonely down here with only these toxic rats."

"Uh, I got lost," I lied. How could I ever explain that I was on Earth while she remained locked in this dungeon? Where was the instruction manual to this game, anyway?

A few hours later the hatch creaked open far above us, sending a stream of light onto the slimy dungeon floor.

"The full moon has risen," the emperor reported. "Yet my daughter continues to be most uncooperative—she has escaped from her room! Now this dungeon and all its inhabitants will be drowned in lava!" Rats squeaked wildly and scampered into hidden crevices. "Minions, empty Lava Vat One into the Infernal Dungeon!"

"Climb those jagged rocks," I said desperately to Eryn. "Maybe we can make it up to that hatch." A bright stream of orange lava spewed out of a pipe jutting from the far dungeon wall, creating a sizzling pool on the floor.

"I said only Vat One!" the emperor bellowed from above. "You fools! What have you done?" Five more pipes spilled lava into the growing pool on the floor, filling the dungeon with steam. The glowing

puddle oozed
toward Eryn and me.
"The wall's too mossy!" she
cried, slipping off the rocks. "It's
impossible to climb!"

A secret door in the wall suddenly sprang open above us. Katie peered out at us.

"Hurry, get in here," Katie said, reaching out her hand. I boosted Eryn into the passageway just as the lava neared my feet. Then they both pulled me to safety and slammed the door shut. Darn! Saved by my girlfriend *again*!

"You fools! You fools!" the emperor's voice

boomed from the distance. "The regulation valve has collapsed! The lava will fill up the entire castle! We must evacuate!"

"I'm not sure I can find my way back," Katie said, shuffling through a pile of maps.

"Follow me," Eryn said. She led us quickly through a dizzying maze of secret tunnels. But soon the lava broke through the dungeon walls, filling the lower regions of the castle and making some tunnels impassable. Desperate, we followed any passageway that took us higher, and we became hopelessly lost in the center of the castle. The lava flowed violently, melting walls and crumbling staircases beneath us.

"Let's try up here," I said urgently, bounding up a tower staircase. The full moon shone through arched windows, so I knew we were close to freedom. Unfortunately, the stairs ended at a locked door.

"Open up! Open up!" Katie hollered, banging on the door. The lava climbed quickly up the stairs, on a mission to devour us. Just as it reached the top step, the door flung open and a figure dressed in black pulled us to safety.

"Michael Bottompockets!" Katie said in surprise as I slammed the door shut behind us.

"At your service, Princess," he said, kneeling. "As if our minds were one, I sensed that you were in trouble, and I spared no time in seeking out the castle and rescuing you."

"Really?" Katie asked, giving Michael a funny look.

"Uh, no," Michael said, slumping his head. "After I told my dad about the metal dragon's head, he sent me here to steal it." He showed Katie the Amulet Base containing the shiny DragonFlame. "But I spared no time in opening the door after I heard you banging."

"We haven't much longer," Eryn said, sweeping away some lava that oozed under the bulging door.

Michael took a weird device out of his bag and ran over to a window. He pressed a button on it, and a grappling hook shot out the end and clamped onto something in the distance.

"Hurry, slide down this," he said, attaching the device to the window frame. "We must get to the dock."

One by one we slid to freedom and climbed into a rickety boat that was moored in the water. As we pushed off into the night, the castle erupted, sending avalanches of rock and lava down the mountainous crag.

"This isn't exactly the plan that my dad and I worked out," Michael said, rowing toward the giant googly-eyed moon in the distance.

After we'd left the molten ruins far behind, the moon opened its mouth and said, "PowerUp Bonus!" My robe turned blue, and Katie's armor changed from copper to brass. This time I got five new spells: *Ice Demonite, Feather Flight, Conjure Q, Add Sides, and Invincible Barrier.* At least these spells sounded a little cooler.

"Fantastic, I got my new thief-only DragonSword," Michael said, swinging around an intricately carved metal handle capped with a one-eyed dragon's head.

While the moon kept an eye on us, Katie and I told Michael about the DragonSteel Amulet quest, but we were careful not to mention anything more about the video game or our true identity as humans. Michael agreed to help us find the rest of the enchanted jewels, as long as he got to keep any other loot that we found along the way.

"Now we have to get to the Eastern Kingdom," I said eagerly. "The Red DragonEye is there."

ERYN LEARNS HER TRUE DESTINY

"A dventure!" Eryn cheered, waving her broom in the air. "It's so wonderful not to be cooped up in that dusty old castle anymore." A calm sea sparkled under the midday sun.

"Instead, we're lost in the Sea of Mirages," Michael said despairingly, looking through a black spyglass. "We drifted aimlessly all night while we slept."

"I don't feel lost around so many great heroes," Eryn said excitedly, jumping around the boat. "There's Princess Ignatia, the rebel warrior who fights for justice and rescues people from certain doom. There's Michael Bottompockets, the mysterious thief dressed in black, who travels the world stealing exotic treasures. There's JuJu, who … Um … Well, you're cute, JuJu, and you have funny spells."

"'Cute' is my favorite adjective," I said sarcastically. How embarrassing—I couldn't even impress a scullery maid!

Suddenly a three-headed serpent burst out of the water and lifted its scaly head high into the air. Michael tried to swipe his DragonSword across its bar code, but he fell right through the creature and splashed into the water.

"Mirage!" Eryn announced, helping Michael back into the boat with her broom.

"I thought that one was real," Michael said, wringing out his mask.

"That's the tenth mirage since daybreak," I complained, slamming down my DragonStaff. "When are we gonna get across this dumb sea?"

We rowed all afternoon, encountering dozens of new mirages. Katie sat near Michael and chatted with him in a secretive voice. She paid no attention to me at all. Grumpy the whole time, I pretended to read my spell book so they wouldn't know I was watching them.

"Mirage!" Michael announced, pointing at a sand-colored palace in the distance.

"I wish it was a real palace," Katie said longingly. "Maybe then we could stop in for dinner."

"Princess Ignatia is hungry," Michael proclaimed, jumping to his feet. "JuJu, summon us some food."

"I don't have any food spells," I said, suddenly realizing I was holding my spell book upside down.

"But you must have *Conjure Q* by now," Michael argued. "That's my favorite thing about magicians."

Confused, I flipped through the spell book until I found *Conjure Q.* Then I activated my finger and pointed at Katie. At once a table appeared, covered with piles of hamburgers, steaks, and ribs. Yuck!

Michael took off his gloves and eyed the food greedily. Just as he prepared to put some on a plate, he said, "Hey, where's the ketchup?"

"Add sides, add sides!" Eryn urged as the table began fading.

I cast *Add Sides* and another table appeared, this one covered with mustard, ketchup, potato salad, and coleslaw. Michael and Eryn breathed a sigh of relief when the barbecue reappeared. With swift hands, Michael grabbed a heaping plateful of food, arranged it nicely, and handed it to Katie, saying, "Your meal, Princess."

That was when I snapped. "I'm officially the lamest, wussiest, most useless character in this dumb game!" I hollered, throwing my spell book down onto the deck. "Why couldn't I have chosen—"

"Where are you taking me, you crazy bird?" a distant voice interrupted. A giant rainbow-colored

bird flew toward us carrying an old man in a basket on its back. "Whoa, Myna." The bird hovered over our boat and pecked at the piles of meat.

"Shoo, shoo," Eryn said, swatting at the bird with her broom.

"You must excuse Myna," the man said. "She's eaten only seaweed and clams for eight hundred years." Myna swallowed all the hamburgers in one gulp and then started on the ribs. "Oh, dear. My most sincere apologies to you, adventurers. You're welcome to stay at the sand palace as a token of my apologies. I'm Fettyl, and I'll be working on the west wiiiiiiiiiiiiing." The bird whisked Fettyl toward the sand palace, nearly dumping him out of the basket.

We paddled over to the majestic palace, which towered out of sight into a white cloud. The entire building, complete with windows, gargoyles, ivy-covered towers, and balconies, was made out of sand. Fettyl sat in his basket repairing a section of the palace with a spoon while Myna flapped steadily in place.

"Head on in," Fettyl said, waving the spoon. "Watch out for that grumpy old wizard in there, though."

We walked cautiously up a sand staircase and through a tall doorway. An enormous sand sculpture of a fluffy dog sat in the center of the foyer. Into one wall was carved a giant map of Komondor, which Michael studied carefully. The fancy etching showed the locations of the three major kingdoms—Western, Eastern, and Northern—along with a mountain range, forest, snowy wasteland, and sea between them.

"Welcome to the sand palace," a green-haired woman said, walking over to us. I'm Mettyl—the only *real* wizard in the Sea of Mirages."

"Did you build this palace?" Eryn asked, pointing her broom at the wall.

"Is that a Broom of the Ancient Healers?" Mettyl shrieked. She ran over to Eryn and snatched the large broom out of her hands. "When I met my husband nine hundred years ago, he came to me with one of these—didn't even know what it was, the knucklehead. How come healers take so long to discover their true identity?" She slammed the broom against a giant clamshell, knocking off the brush and revealing a sparkling crystal at the end of the broomstick.

"Can this really be true?" Eryn asked, waving the staff in the air. A spell book appeared and fell to Eryn's feet. She leaned down and carefully picked it up.

"It's true, dear. Occasionally, when a purple hit-point sphere vanishes, a healer such as yourself appears somewhere in the world," Mettyl explained. "Healers have no parents, and their only worldly possession is a large broom with a crystal hidden away under the brush."

"I've often wondered why I was a scullery maid for the Emperor of the West my whole life," Eryn said.

"He must have found you and raised you as a servant, unaware that your true destiny is to keep others healthy," Mettyl speculated. "How exciting! Our first visitors in nine hundred years, and quite an unusual bunch you are!"

"This palace has been standing for nine hundred years?" I asked while Eryn eagerly flipped through her spell book.

"When my husband and I took this job, the

palace had been standing for five thousand years," Mettyl began. "Legend has it that the great creator, Komondor, dug a giant cwm in the Peaks of Doom, and the excavated sand formed a sky-high mountain in the Sea of Mirages. Komondor placed a mystical bone in the cwm, and over the years, the bone broke apart into twelve enchanted pieces. From those pieces the twelve ancient dragons were born, and when they were old enough, they used their sharp claws to carve the mountain of sand into a great palace. According to the Great Prophecy, this palace will one day be a rest stop for the Chosen Ones, whose destiny it is to restore peace to our world."

"That's just a bedtime story," Michael sneered. "We've all heard it told a hundred different ways. Where's this prophecy written anyway?"

"Why, right here," Mettyl said, pointing at a giant book on a pedestal. Below the title, *The Great Prophecy,* smaller writing said "By Syzygy, Keeper of the Fates." Mettyl flipped through thousands of pages of tiny print while Michael looked on in amazement. Mettyl retrieved a magnifying glass and began reading one particular page closely. "Ah, interesting, interesting. It's been a while since I've consulted the book."

"You mean your whole life is written in a book?"

Katie asked. "You know everything that's going to happen?"

"Most of the text is difficult to interpret," Mettyl said. "Let me share with you an excerpt describing how the Chosen Ones arrive at the sand palace." Mettyl cleared her throat and began reading from the giant book:

Five minions of low intelligence—
Aargh!
Lava brightens the night sky.
Burn, lava, burn.

A boat rescues four:
A boy of darkness

And one of cheesy spells,
A girl of royalty
And one who inside hidden healer dwells.

The sand palace reached through tempting
*   barbecue,*
A big bird, shoo shoo!
The story of Komondor's dragons reveals
*   a disbeliever.*
Mettyl reads and then drops a magnifying
*   glass on her foot!*

"Oh, dear!" Mettyl said in surprise, dropping the magnifying glass on her foot. "I should have known the Chosen Ones were among you! Everyone else passes by, thinking this palace is a mirage. Fettyl, Fettyl, the Chosen Ones! The Chosen Ones!"

She ran outside and told Fettyl the news. Astonished, he fell out of his basket and landed in a pile of Myna's feathers.

That evening Mettyl and Fettyl put Katie, Eryn, and me in a three-room suite in one of the palace towers. Michael had to sleep outside on the feather pile.

"It's so sad that he gets treated like a criminal," Katie said, watching Michael toss and turn far below. Her elbows made indentations in the sandy window frame.

"But he *is* a criminal," I said, knocking the lumps out of my bed.

"He steals things only for important quests," Katie argued. "Like the two amulet pieces that he rescued for us."

"Whatever," I said, plopping onto the mound of dry sand. "I'm going to bed."

"He asked me out, y'know," Katie admitted shyly.

"How did he take the bad news?" I asked, pulling a blanket of seaweed over me.

"Well, um, I kinda said yes," Katie mumbled.

"What!" My head felt like an anvil had fallen on it.

"Oh, we can still be best friends," she said, running over to comfort me. "We've never even kissed anyway, so what's the difference?"

"You never told me you wanted to kiss!" I said, pulling away from her.

"I'm not supposed to *tell* you. It's just supposed to happen, like, naturally," she said, sighing dreamily.

"Well, who cares," I said angrily. "I never wanted to go out with you anyway."

"You're just being a big baby, like always," she

jeered, storming into her adjoining room. She slammed the clamshell partition shut and didn't say another word.

Things couldn't possible get any worse. I was a mutant Japanimation. I had lame spells. I was wanted by the FBI. My girlfriend dumped me for a thief ... I buried my head in the sand and cried myself to sleep.

ON TO THE LAND OF SNOWY MIST

The next morning I woke up when a big chunk of sand fell on me. I rolled over and tried to get comfortable again until I realized that the ceiling was caving in. I leaped out of bed and dashed to the window.

"Produce my daughter and the stolen amulet pieces this instant or I'll destroy another precious tower!" the Emperor of the West threatened. Outside, the emperor sat on a fancy throne supported by giant black birds. An army of minions holding baskets hovered beside him.

"This palace will fulfill its destiny of safely harboring the Chosen Ones!" Mettyl vowed, pointing her finger at the evil army. A lightning bolt zapped one of the minions out of the sky.

"Enough talk! Minions, invade!" the Emperor of the West ordered. Hundreds of wings flapped as a brigade of minions ambushed the palace, whizzing around like planes and dropping snapping crabs out of their baskets. The crabs ate away at the sand, causing the palace walls to crumble. Just when I thought things couldn't get any worse!

"There's a war because of us," Katie said, running into my room. Eryn came in moments later, and the three of us watched in awe as Mettyl and Fettyl bravely defended us. Towers collapsed everywhere, and I imagined getting smushed under a mountain of sand. I grabbed my spell book and furiously looked for any spell that could help.

"Stand still for Ultimate Healing!" Fettyl cried, pointing at Mettyl. The purple sphere above Mettyl grew larger.

"The stairway ... collapsed," Michael panted, running into the room. "I came to rescue you, but I ... already used ... grappling hook ..." He bent down to gasp for air.

"I have a spell that will work!" I announced as the tower trembled. "Everybody put your stuff in Ignatia's magical backpack."

Eryn put in her staff, Michael added his black bag, and I tossed in my DragonStaff. I pointed at the spell *Feather Flight* before putting my book in the pack. Then I waved my hand, turning everybody's arms into white, featherlike wings.

"C'mon," I said, jumping out the window. We escaped into the air just as the entire palace crumbled into a pile of loose sand.

"Go now and restore peace to Komondor!" Mettyl shouted over the noise of the ongoing battle. "You are the Chosen Ones—fulfill your destiny!"

"Follow me," Michael said, flying over the water. "According to that map in the sand palace, the Land of Snowy Mist begins directly to the north. I know the way to the Eastern Kingdom from there."

Katie and Michael soared next to each other, and I stayed near Eryn. Her long purple spike of hair pointed backwards in the breeze.

"See, you have useful spells," Eryn said, tickling me under the arm with the end of her wing. I tickled her back, and pretty soon we were playing a game of flying tag, zooming up and down in complicated maneuvers. Katie and Michael left us far behind.

"I guess being a magician might be OK," I said, circling Eryn. "At least my robe is blue now."

"It's cute," she said, slapping my cheek with her wing. "Y'know, it's written in the Great Prophecy that you're supposed to go out with me."

"Really?" I asked. We stopped playing tag and continued flying north.

"Yeah, I peeked ahead in the book while Mettyl was reading."

"Awesome, let's go out," I said.

"OK," Eryn agreed. I was so happy I almost fell into the water.

A few minutes later the air turned cold, and the Land of Snowy Mist appeared. It looked just like it did in the pictures on the *DragonSteel* card game—giant snowdrifts blowing around in an end-less blizzard. After Eryn and I flew over the white wilderness, our wings iced up, and we spiraled down into the snow.

"What took you so long?" Michael said, shaking some icicles off of his wings. "The princess is cold."

"Why couldn't we have flown to the Land of the Hot Tubs?" Katie asked, running around to warm up.

"Let's get moving. We have to cross the Peaks of Doom," Michael said, pointing at jagged snow-capped mountains in the distance. "My dad once took me through them on a quest."

We silently trudged east, heading for the towering peaks. Somewhere on the other side of them lay the Eastern Kingdom, home of the Red DragonEye. I hoped that the Amulet Base with the Sapphire DragonFlame still lay safely tucked in Katie's backpack. Who could ever have thought that my whole future would depend on a piece of jewelry?

As we hiked over the giant snowdrifts, our wings froze into solid blocks of ice. It figured—my one useful spell, and it gave us all frostbite. I vowed to throw a snowball at the first person who mentioned it, when I had arms again.

"When is this spell going to wear off?" Eryn inquired.

"Soon, soon," I said, smiling anxiously and gritting my teeth. Well, the first person other than Eryn.

I soon realized that hundreds of fuzzy white

puppies were silently frolicking in the snow all around us, nearly invisible against the white background. They burrowed in and out of snowdrifts, playing an endless game of hide-and-seek.

After hours of trekking through this strange snowy wasteland, I heard loud noises from up ahead.

"Dis is deleterious! It catching up to me!" a gravelly voice yelled. It was the English Golem, suddenly appearing at the top of a tall hill! A tiny purple sphere hovered over his head, and he limped awkwardly in our direction. The puppies whimpered and disappeared into the snow.

"Golem!" Michael said. "Run!" We tried to sprint away, but the golem caught up to us in only a few seconds.

"Yur pulchritudinous!" the golem said, towering over Katie and beaming down at her. He batted his eyelashes.

"Wait—this golem doesn't have a bar code," Michael said, walking around it. "It's not evil."

The golem calmly sat down beside Katie, blushing. He pulled a green flask out of a large sack and threw it on the ground, creating a poof of white smoke that made our arms normal again. Eryn retrieved her spell book and cast a healing spell, enlarging the golem's purple sphere.

"Danks fer da heal!" the golem said, awkwardly standing up.

"Anytime, Golem," Eryn said proudly.

Just then a creature ten times larger than a brontosaurus appeared at the top of the hill, covered with sharp icicles. It scowled at us and narrowed its glowing blue eyes.

"Oops, me fergot ice behemoth chasing me," the golem said, retrieving a Wand of Ice Shards from the sack. "Get ready fer prodigious battle."

"JuJu, when the behemoth's eyes glow red, cast *Invincible Barrier*," Michael instructed as the creature tromped down the hill. "Eryn, you heal Ignatia and me when the barrier's up. Golem, don't use your wand until the barrier breaks."

Katie and Michael charged the behemoth, swiping their DragonSwords over its bar code. Sky-high holographic behemoths flew out the end of their sword handles, and sparks flew when Michael and Katie swung them at the beast. The real behemoth had a gigantic purple sphere and heavy armor, but *we* had teamwork. We defended ourselves against icicle missiles, snowball bombs, freezing rays, and avalanches. Our magic lit up the sky like a laser light show, and before long we knocked the behemoth's hitpoints down to a tiny purple sphere.

When Eryn and the golem were out of magic and

the DragonSwords began flickering, I panicked and cast my last spell, *Ice Demonite*. A tiny goblin appeared, ran up to the behemoth, and stuck out its tongue.

"Nyah Nyah," the goblin said, spitting and making rude noises. Enraged, the behemoth charged at the goblin. The goblin shrieked in fear, and the behemoth chased it off into the distance. Everybody's purple hitpoint sphere returned to full size and then vanished.

"What was *that?*" Michael screamed, throwing down his DragonSword. "We were going to win, and behemoths always drop lots of gold and jewels as loot!"

"I didn't know what the spell did," I said, embarrassed.

"You are the worst magician Komondor has ever seen!" Michael said, kicking the snow.

"Fine, then I quit this team!" I hollered, slamming down my DragonStaff. "I'm not casting another spell for anybody!"

"Why dat thief and magician so exasperated?" the golem asked, limping back to his bag. "We win. Da behemoth gone, and all our hitpoints replenished."

"I don't know," Katie said, cleaning off her DragonSword. "I think they're both being big babies now."

"It goes much deeper than that, Golem," Michael began. "JuJu's mad because I stole his girlfriend."

"You did not," I said, glaring at Katie. "I happen to be going out with Eryn." Katie's jaw dropped wide open.

"You come back to Golem cave," the golem said. "Me exultant dat you come along and save Golem. Me feed you, and we play game."

Eryn healed everyone, and then we hiked east in silence until we came to a cave at the foot of the Peaks of Doom. As we entered the lair, a booming voice said, "PowerUp Bonus!" The familiar bubble letters flew around until they froze and fell apart.

"Yay," Eryn cheered. An image of Eryn surrounded by a purple glow appeared in the crystal at the end of her staff. I didn't even look at my new spells because I was too angry to care. I just wanted to finish the quest, get back home, and become normal-looking again—and bring Eryn back too, of course.

WE MAKE A GREAT DISCOVERY

Piles of dictionaries filled the English Golem's cave. One was entitled *The Deluxe Book of Synonyms and Antonyms*. Another read *The Secret Language of Thieves*. In the center of the room sat a giant unabridged dictionary, which the golem used as a table.

After a dinner of mysterious black soup, the golem retrieved five sacks of marbles from a shelf and distributed them. Then he moved the giant unabridged dictionary off to the side and drew a big circle in the dirt.

"Me play marbles dexterously. It Golem's favorite game. Nobody beat Golem ever."

"Golem, you know many big words," Katie said, "but how come you don't study grammar?"

"Me grammar live in da Peaks of Doom," the golem said. "She teach me how to play marbles." He placed all his marbles except one in the circle.

"You takes one marbles to shoot with and puts others in circle. If you hits any marbles out of circle with shooter, you get to keep dem."

All of a sudden I spotted a glowing blue marble in the center of the circle. Weird. When I stared at it, a mysterious feeling of power surged through my body, and I felt like crawling around on my hands and knees.

"That's the Blue DragonEye!" I whispered excitedly to Eryn, elbowing her. She whispered to Katie, who whispered to Michael.

"Golem, where did you get that blue marble?" Katie asked, pointing.

"Dat's Golem's favorite marble. Me gets it from me grammar. It been in family for thousands of years."

"Shoot for the blue, shoot for the blue," I whispered to everyone as we started the game. My legs felt weak from excitement.

"Me rapturous dat yur here," the golem said, shooting his marble. "Me gots not many friends cause everybody make fun of Golem's funny looks." The golem's shooter knocked four marbles out of the circle.

"Well, maybe they don't know that you like to play fun games," I said, rolling my marble. I knocked ten marbles away from the DragonEye, clearing a path to it.

"Just ignore them," Katie suggested, aiming for the eye. She tapped it closer to the edge of the circle.

"Yeah, you're a nice golem," Eryn said, hitting the sparkling blue diamond right onto the circular boundary line.

"I'm gonna get this," Michael vowed, lining up his marble carefully. He launched the shooter marble at full speed, but it missed the DragonEye and hit the golem in the foot. The golem winced, and Michael slumped his head in embarrassment.

"Har har, dis easy shot now," the golem said, casually knocking the Blue DragonEye out of the circle. We all groaned in disappointment.

After a few hours the golem had a mound of marbles in front of him, and we had only a few.

"OK, Golem, you win, but can we pleeeease have that blue marble" I begged, getting on my knees.

"Nope, dis me favorite marble. Me would experience perturbation if me not have it." The golem limped over to the shelf and put his marbles away.

Suddenly I had an idea of how I might trick the golem.

"Golem, let's play a different game," I said, flipping through the giant unabridged dictionary. "If I can guess your favorite word in the whole English language, you have to give me that marble."

"Har har, dat easy game," the golem said. "Dere millions of words. OK, you gets one guess."

"I bet it's 'floccinaucinihilipilification,'" I said, scanning the dictionary's page of longest words.

"Flock-see-know-see-knee ... hilly-pilly-fikay-shun?" the golem said stumblingly, looking at me in awe. "What *dat* mean?"

"Uh, the act of thinking something is worthless," I said, reading the definition. "So when those creatures make fun of you, you just have to practice floccinaucinihilipilification. Then what they say doesn't mean anything." I shut the dictionary and hoped I was right.

"Flock-see-know-see-knee ... hilly-pilly-fikay-shun," the golem sang, clapping his hands. "Me likes da sound of dat!" The golem danced around, repeating the word again and again until he became tongue-tied. Then he groaned, grabbed his foot, and fell onto a pile of dictionaries.

"So, Golem, what's your favorite word in the whole English language?" I asked confidently when we sat in a circle again.

"Hmmm," the golem said, scratching his chin. "Me favorite word is 'cat' because dey so yummy."

I flopped down on my back, utterly disappointed.

"You shouldn't eat cats," Katie scolded. "That's mean."

"What you think in dat soup we ate?"

Ugh. After we went to bed, I tossed and turned most of the night, trying not to think about what I was digesting. Occasionally Michael snuck over to the shelf and tried to steal the Blue DragonEye, but a red light flashed whenever he got near it.

"Me put anti-thief charm on dat marble," the golem said in the middle of the night. "You go backs to sleep now."

In the morning we walked wearily out of the cave into the bright sunlight. The golem limped over to the cave entrance and waved to us.

"Danks fer stopping by," he said, wincing and hopping on one foot. "It nice grouping wit you."

"How come you limp all the time, Golem?" Eryn asked. "Did you hurt your foot?"

"Me have thorn in foot for two years," the golem answered, lifting his foot to show her. "Me can't reach it, and magic potions not efficacious."

"Why didn't you ask us to take it out?" Eryn questioned.

"Me not want to impose."

Eryn ran over to the golem and carefully plucked the long thorn out of his foot. Then she cast a spell that made the wound disappear.

"Wow, me forgot what no pain in foot like," the golem said cheerily. He danced around Eryn, making the icy blubber around his middle wobble. Then he ran into the cave and came out seconds later with the Blue DragonEye! "Me give this to you as thanks. Me not have pain now if it gone."

"Thanks, Golem!" Eryn said, firmly grasping the glowing jewel.

The four of us walked up a twisty path leading into the Peaks of Doom. When the golem was out of sight, Michael handed me the Amulet Base and I placed the Blue DragonEye into the empty slot. While the amulet glowed briefly, my tongue hung limply out of my mouth, and I began panting. Embarrassed, I forced my tongue back in while everybody looked at me strangely.

"We need only the Opal Nostril and Red Drag-onEye now," I said with renewed confidence, staring at the amulet. The fire-breathing steel dragon seemed to wink at me because of its missing eye. "Now let's get to the Eastern Kingdom."

WE CROSS THE PEAKS OF DOOM

This place gives me the creeps," Michael said as we entered an icy ravine.

Soon we were lost in a frozen maze, with steep paths leading in every direction. To make matters worse, ice sloths, glacial bats, and enchanted snowmen attacked us at almost every turn. I stubbornly refused to cast any more spells, so the rest of the group had to fight by themselves. After all, things were starting to go well again, and I didn't want to mess it up by casting some lame spell.

"But JuJu, your magic is helpful in its own way," Eryn argued.

"You're wasting your time," Katie said, glaring at me. "He's too stubborn."

We journeyed through the peaks all day, climbing rickety ladders and jumping over bottomless ravines. My ears popped when an ice elevator brought us to the summit of the tallest peak,

where I glimpsed the Thieves' Forest and the Sea of Mirages far in the distance. At one point I got a PowerUp Bonus, and I hadn't even cast a spell! My robe turned green, and my DragonStaff changed from wood to brass.

At nightfall, we came to a giant crater at the far edge of the peaks. A dilapidated yellow cabin stood next to it, the same one I had seen when Katie and I soared over the mountains at the beginning of the game. A sign over the door read "JuJu's Hut." I peeked through one of the shattered windows. Broken beakers, computer parts, and puddles of chemicals littered the floor inside.

"I didn't know you lived in the Peaks of Doom," Eryn said to me. "It must be lonely here."

"What's this?" Michael asked, picking up a book by the edge of the crater—the exact spot where JuJu sat when Aidan helped me choose my character. "Is this yours, JuJu?" He handed me the book. I opened it, revealing hundreds of pages of diary entries. The latest one read:

The worst has happened. While I was gathering magical ingredients in the Sea of Mirages, someone ransacked my cabin and stole my most prized creation—Interdimensional Schlepp—a magical device that can force a dimensional hole between Komondor and Earth. I fear it was taken by one of the evil beasts from the Northern Kingdom. They are everywhere now, carrying out the emperor's bidding. His fiendish army of slaves worries me greatly—they are unsightly terrors summoned by the Emperor of the North using ancient shards of magical DragonSteel. Will his power go unchecked until all of Komondor falls victim to evil?

That reminds me—I discovered during my travels that one of these beastly armies from the North recently unearthed the legendary

Opal Nostril in the Abysmal Desert while mining for ancient DragonSteel fragments. Tomorrow I shall set out for the Northern Kingdom in an attempt to recover my invention and snoop around. I must prepare well. The technology there is very futuristic and advanced. As well, I heard a rumor that the Emperor of the North has obtained enough DragonSteel to create an evil pet dragon of unspeakable strength. It is said to have the combined power of all the ancient dragons. I sincerely hope that this is not my last diary entry. JuJu.

"When did you write that, JuJu?" Michael asked, peering over my shoulder. "You never told me the Emperor of the North had the Opal Nostril. Are you holding out on us?"

"I didn't know. I've never even seen this book," I said, handing it to Michael. "I wouldn't have played this game if I knew I had to write hundreds of pages."

Michael and Eryn stared at me, puzzled.

We camped for the night by the edge of the crater. Michael took a black orb out of his bag and threw it on the ground, where it exploded into a strong campfire. After a dinner of stale muffins from

JuJu's hut, Katie and I finally explained the truth about everything—the card game, the computer game, Aidan, the FBI, and our transformation into cartoons.

"Princess, I think you've gone too many days without properly resting," Michael said, holding Katie's hand.

"I'm not a princess, and I'm sick of pretending I am in this ... whatever it is!" Katie shouted, pulling away from Michael. "I'm tired and I wanna go home! My dad's probably called in the army by now."

"That fancy tale *would* explain why you know so little about magic," Michael said, glaring at me. "But I know better than to trust anything a magician says. However, if it would make the princess feel better, you may consult Syzygy about it in the morning. Syzygy is all-knowing."

"You mean the guy who wrote that big book?" I asked, frowning at Michael.

"Syzygy is a *girl*," Michael corrected. "As you should know, she lives right down there in the Forbidden Cwm. Listen, you can hear her." A faint snoring rose up from the depths of the crater. "During your lifetime you're allowed to ask Syzygy one question. After that you're forbidden to approach her. That's why they call it the Forbidden Cwm."

"Since Mettyl told me about my past," Eryn

began, "perhaps I should ask Syzygy what my future will bring."

"When I journeyed through here with my dad, I asked Syzygy whether or not I would marry the prettiest girl in Komondor," Michael confessed.

"What did Syzygy answer?" Katie asked.

"She said, 'No,'" Michael responded. "I guess we are defying fate by being together, Princess."

"That's so sweet," Katie sighed. I felt like puking.

"I thought you didn't *want* to be a princess anymore," I sneered at Katie. She stuck her tongue out at me.

I spent a restless night trying to make sense of everything. JuJu's wrecked hut. Interdimensional Schlepp. Aidan's CD. Evil beasts from the Northern Kingdom. Could Aidan really be trusted? Was this a game after all? I tossed and turned, trying to think of the perfect question to ask Syzygy.

THE GARDEN OF NIGHTMARES

In the morning Michael searched for the tunnel leading out of the Peaks of Doom while Eryn, Katie, and I followed a path leading down into the crater. Every few minutes an awful whine blared from below, knocking boulders and ice chunks off the crater wall. We eventually reached a slick black floor littered with toys. We walked carefully through the clutter and found a small girl at the center of the cwm. She had pink spiked hair and giant eyelashes.

"You're Syzygy?" Katie asked, crouching in front of the girl.

Suddenly a bird carrying a doll flew by, and the little girl stretched out her arms toward it, saying, "Dolly, Dolly." Then she whined so loudly that a boulder dislodged from the cliff and rolled toward us, crushing thousands of toys. Eryn pushed me out of the way just in time. Frazzled, I made a mental note *never* to be without a girlfriend.

"Drop that doll!" Katie demanded, throwing a toy at the bird. The bird dropped the doll and flew off.

"Dolly!" the girl squealed in delight when Katie handed it to her. She tossed it randomly into the mess of toys. "I am indeed Syzygy, Keeper of the Fates, the oldest inhabitant of Komondor. You are now forbidden to ask another question for all eternity."

"Oh, no, I didn't mean to ask my question then," Katie said, dejected.

"Syzygy, are Katie and I playing a computer game or what?" I asked.

"This is not a computer game. Komondor is a living planet that shares the same universe space with Earth—a parallel dimension," Syzygy said, retrieving a bottle of milk from the floor. "Many times in Komondor's history, Earthlings have accidentally strayed here through random, unseen dimensional holes. In fact, your first video game designers stumbled here and borrowed ideas from *our* way of life for their games. All that you recognize from Earthly video games—powerups, hitpoints, quests, cartoon characters—those are the basic rules of life on Komondor. Over the eons, countless other elements of Earthly culture have been influenced by Komondor—Velcro, fine literature, technology, language, and Japanese-style cartoons, to name a few. Now *you* may not ask any more questions for all eternity." Syzygy sucked on a rubber pacifier.

"But if this isn't a computer game, then who's Aidan, what's with that CD, and where are the real Ignatia and JuJu?" I asked desperately.

Syzygy stopped sucking on the bottle and gave me an evil stare. "How dare you ask three more questions! Now you shall face the wrath of Syzygy!" She floated into the air and transformed into an enormous rubber ball. The ball launched into the sky until it became a small black dot, and then it rapidly descended toward the crater, casting an ever-growing shadow over us.

"Run!" I cried as a burst of adrenaline entered my legs. Eryn, Katie, and I raced toward the edge of the crater, but the ball impacted with a sonic boom, launching us sky-high. Then we accelerated down at blazing speed until we crashed into a rocky clearing. Broken toys rained down on us. A flock of birds flew down from nearby trees and marched in a circle above my head, chirping. I was never so happy to be a cartoon—the crash hadn't hurt at all.

"The crater gets a little bigger each year," Michael said, helping Katie up. "At least you landed right near the exit."

"Syzygy has an attitude," I remarked, brushing myself off.

"I hope I'm not forbidden to return," Eryn said, picking up her staff. "I never got to ask my question."

"The Eastern Kingdom is just beyond the Garden of Nightmares," Michael explained, leading us into the dimly lit tunnel. "Let's get moving. The garden gets more difficult to cross as the day wears on."

A sign read "*Beware! Garden of Nightmares ahead. Rated the Scariest Place in Komondor by the Journeyer's Guild!*" As we crept along, torches on the tunnel wall illuminated primitive drawings of scary monsters hiding in closets and under beds.

"What did Syzygy say?" Michael asked, clearing away an enormous purple cobweb.

"She told us we're definitely not playing a game," I responded as we continued along. "Then she got all in a huff."

"You keep calling this a game," Michael said. "We've battled the Emperor of the West, crossed the Sea of Mirages, and encountered the English Golem, all to reunite that amulet you seem so concerned about. This is a serious quest! Unless *you're* playing at something, JuJu. You *are* descended from Brucella, after all. Perhaps you're using Princess Ignatia to take over the Western Kingdom!"

"JuJu would never do that!" Eryn protested.

"What is your problem, thief?" I asked. "You're obsessed with this princess thing. She's just a kid from Springs!"

"I'm suspicious, that's all," Michael asserted, grabbing a torch off the wall. "Maybe your ambition goes even higher than that. How do I know you aren't planning to take over the universe?"

"Because we're the Chosen Ones!" I hollered. "You heard what Mettyl said!"

"That's just a story!" Michael yelled back.

Suddenly giant white spiders crawled out of a crevice in front of us and blocked the tunnel. Michael pulled out his thief-net, swung it around, and then hurled it at the spiders, trapping them.

"Wait here," Michael said, dragging the trapped spiders deeper into the tunnel.

"I *knew* this couldn't be a game," Katie whispered to me. "But that means Aidan's been lying to us the whole time."

"Did you say something, Princess of the Precious Western Kingdom?" I sneered.

"Joe, we could be in danger. You have to talk to me."

"OK, OK," I said. "I remembered last night that Aidan's CD was labeled 'I. SCHLEPP'—that's the thing stolen from Juju's hut—Interdimensional Schlepp. We've been using it to travel to this dimension!"

"Do you think Aidan's one of those evil beasts from the Northern Kingdom?" Katie asked.

"He doesn't look like one," I answered. "Although I thought I saw a bar code on him after he rescued us from the FBI."

"But he's only helped us so far," Katie argued. "Evil beasts don't help people."

"The tunnel exit is just around that bend," Michael said when he returned. "When we get to the garden, look only straight ahead. *Don't* turn your head for any reason."

Before long, we emerged from the tunnel into a country meadow under a sunny blue sky. We followed a cobblestone path flanked by rows of colorful wildflowers. A beautiful garden stretched far into the distance on each side, but I followed Michael's advice and stared straight ahead. It *was* another good opportunity to hold Eryn's hand.

"We're almost to the slide," Michael said after a while. "That's the only good thing about the Garden of Nightmares."

Soon I heard odd noises to my left. Repeatedly,

a grinding sound followed a faint, high-pitched shriek. I squeezed Eryn's hand and stared at the back of Michael's head, thinking about my confusing social life. How would I tell Mom and Dad that my new girlfriend came from a parallel world? Or that she had blue hair? I planned to kiss Eryn next time we were alone, just so she wouldn't break up with me, too.

"Ha ha, Guano, look at that stuffing fly!" Bantam cheered. The grinding and shrieking noises grew much louder now.

"Don't look, whatever you do, don't look!" Michael commanded, hurrying along the path. "We're almost through!"

"Help me, Joe," Snuffles cried in a faint voice. I looked to my left without thinking. A giant conveyor belt sat in the middle of the manicured garden, and all my stuffed bears were strapped to it. The moving belt brought the bears, one by one, into a giant rotating blade that shredded them in seconds. Inches away from certain doom, Snuffles struggled to untie himself with his fluffy white paws.

"Guano think running stuffy-mincer easier den guarding bridge," Guano said, pressing a button on a control box to speed the conveyor up.

"Noooooooooooo!" I cried, running toward the machine, crushing flowers under my feet. Snuffles flew into the rotating blades and showered like confetti all over Bantam.

"JuJu, close your eyes!" Michael yelled.

Suddenly the entire scene shattered like a broken mirror, and the pieces rained to the ground. The sky turned dark and stormy, and I was standing before a giant purple blob covered with eyeballs. It gurgled from various mouths, oozing toward me with a splootching noise.

"That's Blobbo, Keeper of the Garden!" Michael shouted. "Run!"

Poor Snuffles! I sprinted back, and we all ran toward a funnel-shaped opening in the stone wall at the end of the path. Blobbo steamrolled straight for us, swallowing sunflowers and cobblestones.

A sign labeled "Exit Slide" hung over the opening, and a cardboard cutout of the English Golem with an outstretched arm stood next to it. A bubble came out of the golem's mouth, containing the words "You must be dis tall to ride dis slide." Eryn arrived at the opening first and measured herself under the golem's arm.

"Eryn, jump in!" I ordered as Blobbo formed into a giant wave behind me. We dove into the funnel, which narrowed into a slick tubular slide that wound through the depths of Komondor. No roller coaster could even come close to this blazing ride— we flew out of the tube and soared over a lava pool, only to funnel back into the slide on the other side. Then we launched into the center of a cavern, where bursts of air separated us into different tubes that dangerously snaked through each other. Blobbo followed at full speed, determined to devour us.

Finally, the slide spewed us onto a giant pillow on a rocky ledge. A glass staircase led up to a floating crystal palace in the distance.

"Hurry, get up here," Michael said, hopping onto the stairs. "The blob can't adhere to glass."

As we clambered up the staircase, Blobbo burst out the slide's exit. When it saw the crystal palace it groaned in disappointment and slowly oozed back into the mountainside. Another close call. I grabbed Katie's hand for comfort, and Eryn gave me a dirty look.

"Oops," I said, dropping Katie's hand and grabbing Eryn's.

WE MEET PRINCE KIVIN

All of us got a PowerUp Bonus on the glass staircase. Katie's armor turned to steel, Michael received an invisibility potion, and Eryn got a spell that allowed her to create a reflective barrier. My robe turned red, and a gold crown appeared on the head of my DragonStaff. I wanted to peek at all my new spells, but I kept my book shut so nobody would think I went back on my refusal to fight.

"How does this place stay up?" Katie asked as we neared the floating crystal palace.

We walked through a dilapidated gate and approached the entrance. Holes riddled the palace walls, and shards of broken glass lay everywhere.

"Weird, the palace is wrecked and *we* haven't even been here yet," I said, walking inside.

We entered a large foyer containing a tremendous chandelier. A hooded figure stood at the top of a grand staircase.

"The Evil Emperor of the East!" Michael announced, pointing at the figure.

"Hardly," the woman said, walking down the staircase.

Just then a Tarzan scream came from above and a blue-haired boy jumped off the balcony and dangled from the chandelier. He climbed up and sat on it like a swing, swaying back and forth.

"Look, no hands," the boy said, holding up his arms. The chandelier loosened slightly from the ceiling.

"Prince Kivin must always make a dramatic entrance," the figure said, removing her hood. "I'm Empress Grisette. Welcome to the Eastern Kingdom."

"You mean you're not the Evil Emperor of the East?" Eryn asked. Kivin yanked some crystals off the chandelier and threw them at us.

"There is no Evil Emperor of the East," Grisette said, leading us away from the chandelier. "It's a terrible misunderstanding. Whenever anybody comes to my palace, Kivin makes such an awful impression that I've been branded as evil. I have no bar code."

"But why do you wear the black hood?" Michael asked. Kivin did a flip off the chandelier and landed near us.

"I'm embarrassed to show my face, even to my servants. My son is at that awkward level—he's so rebellious, and I just can't convince him to power up. It's been ages since his last PowerUp Bonus, and he just keeps becoming more unruly. That's why I arranged that marriage alliance with your father, Ignatia. Surely that powerful man would have helped my boy power up, but alas, the emperor was defeated in a battle in the Sea of Mirages."

"I'm gonna show you my toy room," Kivin said,

grabbing Eryn's hand and dragging her down a hallway.

"The rest of you may as well go see the toy room," Grisette sighed. "Kivin just *has* to show it to everyone."

We followed Kivin to an immense domed room filled with fancy toys. A bottomless pit lay in the middle of the room, leading to the blue sky below the palace.

"I'm a minstrel," Kivin said, pulling some instruments out of a velvet bag. He played a flute, which magically lifted everybody into the air. "Banzai!" We crashed to the ground in a heap, cracking the glass floor slightly.

"I haven't met many minstrels in my journeys," Michael commented, brushing himself off.

"My great uncle built me this place," Kivin said, grabbing a joystick off the floor. "He's a gnome inventor." He pressed some buttons on the joystick, and a large glass sphere rose out of the bottomless pit. A door in the sphere popped open. "Who wants to ride the Gnomish Yo?" Kivin asked. "It's my favorite ride."

"We will," I said, pulling Eryn into the glass sphere—a perfect opportunity to be alone with her.

"Hope ya like it," Kivin said, fiddling with the controls. The door closed, and the sphere descended into the pit, taking us for a leisurely ride through the core of the glass palace.

"This is fun," Eryn said as we entered the blue sky under the palace. When the building was out of sight above us, I leaned over and tried to kiss Eryn. Suddenly the glass sphere shot upward, flattening Eryn and me on its floor like pancakes. We zoomed up into Kivin's room, and then the sphere dropped back through the pit, squashing us against its glass ceiling. Up, down, up, down we boomeranged until I felt sick.

"Ha ha!" Kivin teased when he finally released us. "It's a Gnomish *Yo-Yo*! I left out the second 'Yo' so you wouldn't be afraid to ride it!" He picked up a harmonica and blew into it, making himself disappear. "Catch me if you can!"

Kivin proceeded to show us every strange toy he had, including one called a Gnomish Superball, which is too painful to describe. After a few hours Eryn, Michael, Katie, and I lay exhausted on the floor.

"Mom, Mom, can I adventure with my new friends? Pleeease?" Kivin asked when Empress Grisette walked in.

"Do you really mean it?" Grisette marveled, kneeling in front of Kivin and holding his hand.

"Yep, I'll even get a PowerUp Bonus, I promise," he said, hugging her.

"How wonderful!" Grisette exclaimed. "If you let my son join your group, I'll give you the Red DragonEye as a reward." She opened a locket around her neck and took out the glowing ruby.

"Fantastic!" Michael said, taking the jewel and handing it to me. "We can use a minstrel in our group. Our magician's on strike."

I snapped the Red DragonEye into the corresponding slot on the Amulet Base, creating a loud hum. Then a bizarre thing happened. I smelled hundreds of new scents around me, and I started sniffing Katie's arm. She swatted me away and gave me a peculiar look. When the humming stopped, my sense of smell returned to normal.

"All we need now is the Opal Nostril!" I said excitedly. "And the Emperor of the North has it."

"You may set out for the Northern Kingdom in the morning," Grisette said. "I insist that you be well rested and properly fed before you take my son on an adventure."

That night Empress Grisette gave us a great feast, and then she tucked us all into the Gnomish Snoozing Machine—a giant ferris wheel with soft compartments to sleep in. All night my bed slowly rotated around the palace, even out into the night sky for some fresh air. It sure beat sleeping in a rickety boat, a lumpy sand bed, a smelly golem cave, or the rocky ground next to a giant crater.

Still, I stayed awake for a long time, wondering when I would see my parents again and what our journey to the Northern Kingdom would bring. If this really wasn't a game, would the completed DragonSteel Amulet still return Katie and me to normal, just as Aidan promised? Or would we transform into the most divine creature in the universe, like the prophecy foretold?

WE HEAD FOR THE NORTHERN KINGDOM

Y ou must all be very careful," Grisette said the next morning, packing Kivin's velvet bag. "My spies just reported that the Emperor of the North is planning an attack on Earth. A beastly army awaits his command in the Northern Kingdom, and the Emperor is on Earth right now establishing his headquarters. He took with him his most powerful brute—a magical dragon of monumental strength!" She brought us to a door leading out the northern side of the palace.

"We'll be careful, Mom," Kivin promised as we started down a glass ramp that stretched into the distance.

"Bye, honey!" Grisette said, waving. "Don't forget to empty the spit out of your instruments!"

We journeyed down the glass ramp all morning. Eventually the glass palace faded into the distance, and only blue sky was visible all around us.

We had to walk carefully because the narrow ramp had no side rails.

At one point Kivin turned to Eryn and said, "Will you marry me?"

"You mean I can be a princess now?" Eryn said excitedly. "Only a few days ago I was a scullery maid!"

"Hey! She's *my* girlfriend!" I insisted. "I should get to marry her."

"Too bad—I asked her first," Kivin declared, holding Eryn's hand.

"Oh, it's OK, isn't it, JuJu?" Eryn asked, turning to me. "We can still be best friends. Anyway, we never even kissed, so what's the difference?"

"That's it, I quit!" I hollered, slamming down my DragonStaff. The impact left a crack in the glass ramp.

"You already quit fighting," Michael said. "You can't quit again. Now who wants to help me split up these gold coins that I swiped from the palace?" He held out a sack.

"You robbed the empress?" Katie said angrily. At that moment the crack spread down the entire length of the ramp, accompanied by a tinkling noise.

"Don't worry, I always rob from the rich and give to the poor, Princess," Michael said, biting one of the gold coins. "And my mom's poor, so it works out fine."

Abruptly the ramp crumbled away beneath us. We all looked at each other in surprise for a few seconds and then plummeted into the blue sky below.

"Me to the rescue!" Kivin announced, reaching into his velvet bag and pulling out his flute. When he played it, we were able to walk in mid-air toward the Northern Kingdom. By the time we arrived at a computerized gate on a rocky cliff, Eryn had finished breaking up with me and Katie had dumped Michael for being a two-bit thief—no doubt making this the first double airborne breakup in history. I was overjoyed about Katie's breakup and angry about being dumped, so I just had a blah feeling.

"My mom was right about this place," Kivin said, pointing through the gate. "Look!" Ghoulish terrors marched back and forth, leaving deep footprints in the dirt—hairy giants, hulking wart-covered lizard-men, multi-headed hunchbacks, and a fanged cyclops. A modern-looking mansion sat on a hill in the distance, covered with antennas and satellite dishes. A digital sign on the gate read "YOU ARE NOT WELCOME IN THE NORTHERN KINGDOM."

Suddenly dark clouds appeared overhead, and thunder boomed. A gray rectangle fell from the sky and crushed the gate in front of us. It contained the words "THIS PROGRAM HAS PERFORMED AN ILLEGAL OPERATION AND WILL BE SHUT

DOWN." Icons labeled "OK" and "CLOSE" sat underneath.

"They've seen us!" Eryn cried, pointing at the monsters. The beasts stomped in our direction, snarling.

"Everybody hold hands!" I cried as giant shadows fell over us. "We're getting outta here!" I hit the "OK" button with my chin while we all held on to each other.

At once, Katie, Michael, Eryn, Kivin, and I appeared as cartoons in the FBI office where Aidan had taken us. Red letters on the computer screen read "ERROR—NOT ENOUGH MEMORY." Agents swarmed through the hallway outside, mumbling into walkie-talkies.

"Where are we?" Eryn whispered as I snatched the CD out of the computer.

"Earth," Katie answered. "Watch out for the FBI. We'll never finish the quest if they find us."

"So this is Earth," Michael marveled, looking around. "It's not at all like my dad described. I don't know what dark magic you're up to, JuJu, but I hope you know what you're doing."

"This place smells," Kivin said, holding his nose.

I wondered if we would get captured by monsters if I stuck the CD right back into the computer. How would we get the Opal Nostril from the

Northern Kingdom unless we got back there? Before I could do anything, an FBI agent ran into the room and spotted us.

"Located escapees in Office 7H," the man announced into his walkie-talkie. "And boss, you were right—there are more of 'em."

"At last!" Agent Alderman said, running into the room, panting. "We've been searching for days."

"I knew there were more of you!" Agent Brasch shouted, peeking into the office. "How many other Gookimunklings are coming?"

"Twelve million," I answered sarcastically. "We're taking over this planet." Agent Brasch looked at Alderman in horror, and then he ran shrieking down the hall.

"Don't mind Agent Brasch," Alderman said. "He always thinks *something*'s taking over the world. Last week it was flying squirrels from the planet Nydor 7. We're taking you back to Springs in the chopper. Follow me."

"I'm not going anywhere until I make a phone call," I said firmly, crossing my arms. Katie also crossed her arms. Eryn, Michael, and Kivin crossed their arms too.

Alderman handed me a cell phone and said I could make the call on the way to the chopper.

"Mom, it's Joe," I said as we marched toward the

roof, escorted by dozens of FBI agents. "We just need to find the Opal Nostril, and then I'll be home."

"Where are you?" Mom sobbed. "The FBI won't tell us anything." I heard Dad crying in the background.

"Tell Dad not to cry," I said. "I'm fine, but I'm still a Japanimation."

"Your father and I just discovered another problem here," Mom said in a serious tone. "We misinterpreted our assignment. We were supposed to make the Acropolis look exactly like it does *now*, not how it looked in the fifth century B.C. Our supervisor's arriving in only a few hours. Oh, Joe, I've never seen your father this upset."

"But you're supposed to be worried about *me*!" I cried. "Who cares about a bunch of buildings!"

"No calls while we're in the air," a tall FBI agent said, taking my phone and lifting me into the helicopter. A few minutes later we were soaring toward Springs. Eryn, Kivin, and Michael stared out the window in awe. Katie grabbed my hand and held it tightly, and everything bad that had happened between us on Komondor suddenly vanished from my mind.

"We found you just in time," Alderman said. "There's a terrible emergency. The FBI needs your help badly."

WE BATTLE AN ANCIENT DRAGON

A snarling, hissing, fire-breathing cartoon dragon was occupying the roof of Springs School. The creature's tail snaked off the side, blocking traffic on School Street. Trapped children stared fearfully out the classroom windows.

"Can your extraterrestrial powers help with this?" Alderman shouted over the hum of the rotors. The helicopter landed in a soccer field behind the school. Our group hopped out and walked toward the building.

"JuJu and the Empress were right!" Michael gasped. "It's the Emperor of the North's evil dragon!"

"Why is it sitting on the school?" I asked dazedly, staring in awe at the colossus. Puffs of smoke curled out of its nostrils.

"Joe, you have to use your magic now," Katie said sternly, readying her DragonSword. "My sister's in there."

"So is Mr. O," I added, opening my spell book. I sat down and studied its pages while Michael searched for the dragon's bar code with his spyglass. I had ten new spells from powering up.

"They told me you were the only ones—the only ones who could h-h-help," Principal Brumby stuttered, hurrying over. Soot covered his cheeks, and burn holes riddled his shirt.

"We'll take it from here," I said confidently as the beast breathed fire.

Six purple spheres appeared in the air. The one above the dragon looked like a small planet.

"Ignatia and I will swipe our DragonSwords," Michael said. "Kivin, help us."

"Roar!" Kivin said, scrunching up his face while pointing at the dragon. "We'll get you, beast!" He took a pair of cymbals out of his velvet bag and smashed them together, turning the overgrown lizard to stone. Ignatia and Michael swiftly climbed up a drainpipe, swiped their DragonSwords over the creature's bar code, and flipped backward onto the ground. Sky-high virtual dragons emerged from their sword handles.

"Casters, announce your spells so we can plan our attacks!" Michael directed as Kivin's spell wore off. The dragon emitted a fiery bellow that shattered the school windows.

"Get off our school!" Katie demanded, zapping the monster with her sword. The dragon lifted its tail and engaged in frenzied swordplay with Katie and Michael, angrily breathing fireballs whenever its purple sphere got smaller.

I cast *Divine Intelligence II* on myself. Immediately a flurry of new ideas flew through my head— the meaning of life, the answers to my girl problems, how to play cribbage. I planned to write all that cool stuff down later. For now, I focused on the only spell combos that could work against such a powerful creature. I activated two fingers and approached the dragon.

"*Conjure Q II!*" I hollered, pointing at the school as Katie and Michael batted fireballs away with their swords. A bed of hot coals appeared under the dragon, melting its purple sphere slightly and forcing the titan to fly into the air.

"*Supreme Boredom!*" I announced, pointing at the dragon. Immediately Mr. O floated out the back door of the school and hovered next to the beast.

"You know, dragon," Mr. O said as the monster glanced at him curiously, "the word 'dragon' is the root of many modern words. There's 'dragon tree,' for instance, which is a tree of the agave family, native to the Canary Islands. Its variegated foliage is probably one of the most ..." The dragon fell asleep and plummeted onto the hot coals, and its purple sphere shrank more.

When my spell wore off and the coals disappeared, the dragon's eyes turned blue, and it angrily sent a ray of ice in my direction.

"*Reflective Barrier!*" Eryn announced, pointing at me. A giant mirror appeared, deflecting the ray back at the dragon, freezing it instantly.

"*Discord of Doom!*" Kivin cried, taking a violin out of his bag. He played terrible screeching notes, which made bits of the dragon's frozen purple sphere crack off. But soon the dragon began to thaw, and its eyes turned an angry red.

"Do you dare think you can defeat *me*?" it sneered in a gravelly voice. "I am the most powerful dragon in the universe, constructed from the metallic remains of all the dragons that came before me! The Emperor of the North created me to protect him, and protect him I will!"

Its eyes glowed purple, and an invisible force wrenched our equipment away like a powerful magnet. A glowing bubble near the dragon's belly soon imprisoned our spell books, DragonSwords, and Kivin's magic velvet bag. Then the creature waved its tail, creating an overgrown Pac-Man that bounced over to our purple spheres and munched them down to tiny dots.

"We're not strong enough!" Katie shouted as the Pac-Man vanished.

"What a great time for thievery," Michael said, pulling the invisibility potion out of a secret compartment in his pants. He drank it and instantly disappeared! Leaving only a trail of footprints, Michael walked over to the school. Then, while the dragon looked around in confusion, he climbed the creaking drainpipe, grabbed the stolen equipment out of the glowing bubble, and brought it all back to us.

"*Group Heal!*" Eryn announced when she held her spell book again. She waved her hand, and our purple spheres grew larger.

"Stubborn creatures," the dragon sneered. "Let us see how your lowly magic can handle this. *Metallic Fury!*" The beast turned to steel. Large metal spikes rose from its skin, and its tail turned into a wrecking ball. The steel dragon leaped into the air and swung the ball at us, but we dove out of the way just in time. The wrecking ball crashed into the earth and showered us with dirt.

I stayed on the ground and activated five fingers with spells while the members of my group bravely defended themselves. Again and again the beast swung its massive tail, but their fancy magic and swordplay fought it off, making the schoolyard look like a busy carnival. The dragon retreated back to the roof, and its eyes turned bright yellow.

"*Rain of Nettles!*" the dragon cried. Immediately its metallic spikes launched into the air, zoomed in our direction, and sliced our purple spheres to bits.

"*Gloom Nebula!*" it bellowed. Before Eryn could cast another healing spell, a cloud of black smoke enveloped us in darkness. Everyone fell around me, coughing. I held my breath, waiting for just the right moment to cast my spells.

"Game *over!*" the dragon uttered confidently,

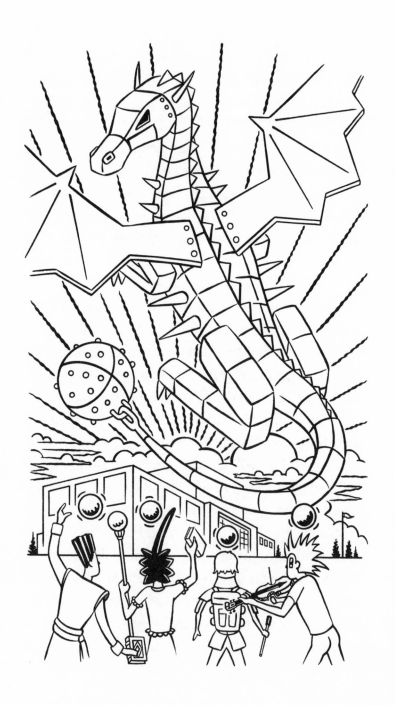

jumping off the roof and causing the ground to tremble. It clomped toward us, snorting.

I rolled out of the black cloud, stopping near the dragon's giant metal foot. When the brute lifted its tail one last time, ready to swing through the black cloud, I pointed at its belly.

"*Containment Orb!*" I yelled. The dragon lurched into the air, where a shiny bubble imprisoned it. Its massive tail harmlessly struck the inside of the bubble.

"*Fiendish Weather!*" I wailed, aiming at the bubble. A black cloud formed inside, sending acid rain onto the metallic dragon until it rusted through. The dragon looked at itself with concern.

"*Big Bang!*" I screamed, pointing at the rusty dragon. A lightning bolt zapped the fragile metal into a million pieces, which crashed against the sides of the bubble. The monster's purple sphere turned to dust.

"*Singularity!*" I announced. The bubble slowly collapsed until it disappeared in a tiny flicker of light.

An eerie silence fell upon the schoolyard as hundreds of children and teachers looked at me in awe through the shattered school windows. I stared in disbelief—we had defeated the dragon, and I hadn't even used my last activated finger. The black cloud surrounding my group disappeared. Katie ran over to me, pulled me to my feet, and gave me a hug. Then, without any warning at all, we kissed!

"Hey, no public displays of affection on school grounds!" the principal ranted, running straight for us. I pointed at Brumby with my last charged finger, casting *Monkey Business* and causing him to slip on a giant banana peel. All the kids cheered. Then a plane flew by carrying a banner that read "PowerUp Bonus!" My robe turned solid gold.

"Yay!" Kivin cheered. "Mom's gonna be so happy! I finally powered up!"

"My parents will *never* believe this," Michael said, removing his mask.

Children soon flowed out the back door of the school and crowded around us.

"You're the greatest superhero ever!" a little boy told me, hugging my leg. Other little kids reached out for me. I stood bewildered, dumbfounded, flabbergasted—I was a hero to the kids, just like I'd always imagined.

Before I could even sign an autograph, a storm cloud appeared in the distance above Springs Hill and erupted in a chorus of thunder and lightning.

WE COMPLETE THE AMULET

Something strange is happening over there," Michael said, pointing at Springs Hill.

"This is another job for *me*," Kivin said. He waved good-bye to the kids and then pulled a shiny kazoo out of his velvet bag. When he blew into it, the five of us were instantly transported to the base of Springs Hill. A long stone staircase led up to the Acropolis, where black clouds exploded in anger.

We slowly climbed up and walked through the giant archway into the main part of the Acropolis. The marble pillars and elaborate carvings made me feel like I had traveled back to ancient Greece. Mom and Dad were pretty good at building stuff, even if they didn't think so.

"Why is there a storm over only *this* hill?" Katie asked as we followed a path toward the Parthenon.

"Because you made me angry," Aidan said,

appearing on the Parthenon's steps in a black cloak and hood. "And I always make clouds when I'm angry."

"You've been lying to us the whole time, haven't you?" I shouted.

Aidan didn't answer. He just tossed a black jewel to me. "Here's the Opal Nostril. Why don't you finish the amulet?" he sneered.

I quickly placed the opal into the last remaining slot on the Amulet Base, hoping to end this crazy journey. A hole opened in the black clouds, sending a ray of sunshine onto me. The completed DragonSteel Amulet emitted a monstrous roar, making me growl, drool, and scratch uncontrollably for a few seconds.

"I am the Emperor of the North!" Aidan admitted. "I tricked you into reuniting the amulet pieces! The Great Prophecy says that only the two Chosen Ones from Earth could do it! Ha!"

"Then why do *you* want the amulet?" I asked.

"The prophecy doesn't say anything about who can *use* the amulet's power once the pieces have been assembled!" Aidan said, walking down the steps. "And I'm the only one who knows how to read the ancient inscription. Ha again!" He reached for the amulet.

"Stop right there!" I said. "I'll cast on you!"

"I suppose you think you can defeat me like you did my pet dragon!" Aidan sneered. "I spent years gathering enough DragonSteel to create her. That building down there made the perfect nest for her, but you had to go and ruin everything!"

I opened my spell book and put my finger on *Time of Ages*. I pointed at Aidan, but he ducked out of the way, and my spell coated the entire Acropolis in a layer of moss and grime.

"Nice try," Aidan said. "I guess by now you've figured out that I'm a powerful enchanter. How do you think I conjured up the *DragonSteel* card game and that store in the mall to find you? Now give me the amulet!" He waved his hand, and a strong wind whipped up.

Our group ran into the Parthenon for safety, but a lightning bolt blew the roof right off. We played a game of cat-and-mouse with Aidan over the entire Acropolis, casting spells and then ducking for cover. Katie and Michael tried to get close enough to Aidan to swipe their DragonSwords. It was no use—he was just too powerful. Pretty soon the Acropolis lay in ruins, and Aidan held the amulet in his hand.

"At last the DragonSteel Amulet is mine!" he said, holding it in the air. "And now, as the Great Prophecy says, I'm going to become the most divine

creature in the universe! With the merest blink of an eye, I'll force legions of people to do my bidding!"

"Give that back! We did all the work!" I demanded, throwing the CD at Aidan. "You just gave us this stupid CD!" It hit him and fell to his feet.

"I don't need it back," Aidan said, kicking the CD. "I have a hundred more copies. They're the only way to force a good, solid passage between Komondor and Earth—*if* you have enough computer memory."

"At least tell us how Katie and I became these characters," I insisted, looking at my cartoon body.

"I used a powerful enchanter spell called *Ruthless Copy*," Aidan explained, polishing the amulet. "Whenever I cast it in Komondor, the victim becomes imprisoned in my dungeon. Then I can transform any Earthling into my captive's exact duplicate. The spell takes a while to stick, but it lasts a long time."

"You're evil!" Katie screamed.

"Duh, I have this," he said, lifting up his sleeve to fully reveal the bar code I had glimpsed earlier. "I only made up the name Aidan because it sounded more innocent than 'Evil Emperor of the North.' That's one thing I don't get about humans—you can't tell who's good and who's evil. I'm gonna take over this feeble planet in like a week. Here goes." He read the ancient inscription that surrounded the perimeter of the amulet. "Rufus Fluffy Shadow Spot, Scruffy Whitey Barney Rover!"

The black clouds disappeared, and Aidan floated into the air, laughing menacingly. A giant paw descended through the atmosphere and tapped Aidan on the head with a bone, creating a brief explosion of white smoke. When the air cleared, Katie and I were human again! The amulet had vanished, and so had Aidan. A fuzzy white puppy sat on a floating pillow in his place. The puppy was a tiny little thing, the cutest dog I had ever seen. He tilted his head and gave me a confused look.

"Roar!" Kivin cried, pointing at Aidan. "We've

got you now!" He pulled a tuba and a xylophone out of his bag. Aidan whimpered in fright.

"No," Eryn said, pulling the instruments away from Kivin. "He's just a puppy."

"Aw, minstrels never get to do finishing combos," Kivin complained.

Michael was staring at Katie and me in amazement. "So you *are* human after all," he said. "You were entangled in the Emperor of the North's diabolical plan."

"You thieves catch on fast," I said sarcastically, pinching myself to see if I really was human. Yes— I could feel real pain again! My regular old clothes were back. My spell book and staff, gone. I was *normal* again, at last!

Just then Mom and Dad, accompanied by a group of women wearing black suits, walked through the entranceway. I grabbed the puppy and ran over to them.

"Joe!" Mom shrieked, hugging me. Tears ran down her cheeks.

"You're back to normal!" Dad said, putting his arm around me.

"Mom, Dad, can I keep this puppy we found?" I asked, pulling away from them.

But just then Mom looked up and saw the buildings around us. Her hands flew to her mouth. Dad fell to his knees and stared at the Acropolis in shock. That was when it occurred to me that I had wrecked their most prized creation. I slumped my head in shame as everybody gawked at the ruins in silence.

"Brilliant," one of the women said at last, staring at the rubble. "The way you've recreated two thousand years of weathering on the outside of these stones is remarkable."

"And the natural manner in which all the ruined stones rest upon one another is outstanding," another added.

"This is an extraordinarily faithful copy of the

Acropolis today," the third woman said. "When you said the project didn't fit our specifications exactly, I didn't know it *exceeded* them."

My spirits soared—I wasn't going to be banished from society! As Mom and Dad looked at each other in confusion, Aidan jumped out of my arms and ran over to Dad's feet. Dad immediately turned his attention to the puppy.

"You're a cute little thing, aren't you, oh yes you are," Dad said in a cutesy voice, leaning down and picking Aidan up. He completely forgot about the inspectors.

"He's simply *divine!*" one of the inspectors said, scratching Aidan under the chin. Aidan blinked one eye.

"He blinked an eye!" another inspector said. "What do you suppose that means? Perhaps he wants a cracker?" She reached into her bag, pulled out a cracker, and fed it to Aidan. Pretty soon Mom, Dad, and all the inspectors were crowded around the puppy and had forgotten about the Acropolis.

"So *that's* what the prophecy meant," Michael said. "You have to be careful with ancient prophecies."

PEACE IS RESTORED

M om, Dad, I'll be back later," I said, picking up the CD. "I have to return my friends to a parallel dimension."

"OK," Dad said absent-mindedly, playing with the puppy.

"Don't forget to look both ways," Mom added, rubbing Aidan's belly. She pushed one of the inspectors out of the way to get closer to the puppy.

"Everybody, follow me," I commanded, walking into the Visitors' Center, the only building not damaged by our fight with Aidan. A bunch of computers flashed information about ancient Greece. I popped the CD into one of them, and we were immediately back at the wrecked gate to the Northern Kingdom. Katie and I were now humans in the cartoon world. The hideous beasts were gone, replaced by scattered pieces of misshapen DragonSteel. Aidan's mansion was a pile of rubble.

"What happened?" JuJu's voice asked from amidst the ruins.

"I don't care," Ignatia's voice said. "I'm just glad to be out of that wretched dungeon."

The *real* Ignatia and Juju, who had been ruthlessly copied and imprisoned in Aidan's dungeon, wandered over to us. They were covered in black soot.

"We defeated the Emperor of the North," I announced. "So his kingdom fell, and the *Ruthless Copy* spell broke. You're free!"

"Well done!" JuJu praised, patting me on the back. "For a human."

"Tell us the whole story," Ignatia said. "I'm eager to find out what befell my evil father."

"We'll tell you later," Kivin said, pulling the kazoo out of his bag. "We're going back to my palace now." He blew into the kazoo, and at once all seven of us found ourselves in the foyer of the glass palace.

"You're back!" Empress Grisette said excitedly, running over and hugging Kivin.

"Mom, Mom, I powered up," Kivin said, opening his velvet bag. "Look, I got a piano!" He pulled out a grand piano and began pounding on the keys. Shards of broken glass floated up and repaired the palace walls, chandelier crystals reattached themselves, and all the dirt disappeared. After a few minutes the palace looked brand-new.

"Wonderful!" Empress Grisette exclaimed, looking around in surprise.

"We defeated the Emperor of the North," Kivin continued. "And I'm gonna marry Eryn."

"Now that the Emperors of the North and the West are out of the way, you are sole ruler of Komondor, Empress," Michael said.

"What a wonderful job you've all done! My son loves adventuring again, and peace has been restored to our world! I'll throw a huge party and invite every non-evil resident of Komondor!"

Katie and I fell back to Earth when Dad shut off the main power to the Acropolis. I hid the CD in my pocket, and we ran out to meet my parents before they left. Mom and Dad had never looked happier. I was back to normal. The Acropolis was a success. We had a cute puppy. Best of all, I wasn't grounded.

We had no school for the rest of the month while the FBI conducted an investigation and the school was repaired. As word spread about the cutest puppy in the world, people lined up at our door with dog biscuits, hoping to get a glimpse. He soon became more popular than the Acropolis as a tourist attraction. After visiting Aidan, Katie's parents even let me hang out with her again. Aidan really did control legions of people!

On the day school reopened, Principal Brumby let Katie and me skip class to take a special tour of the school with the visiting Chancellor of Education.

"I'm glad to see that Springs School has recovered nicely from that, uh, supernatural incident," the chancellor said as we walked down a hallway.

"Indeed, everything is back to normal," the principal proudly reported. "Thanks to our two heroes, of course."

"Yep, I guess we don't have to go to school anymore," I said confidently, reaching for Katie's hand. Brumby scowled and stepped between Katie and me.

"I'm very impressed," the chancellor said, pushing open the door to the schoolyard. He looked outside and immediately froze in shock. On the soccer field dozens of kids wearing colorful robes ran around pretending to cast spells.

"Blob of Snot!" Max yelled, pointing at Eric. Eric pretended to be hit and rolled around in the grass.

"Snot Antidote!" Nikki announced, zapping Eric. Max gave Nikki an evil stare.

"Rain of Chlorophyll!" Eric cried, throwing grass at Max. They soon got embroiled in a friendly grass fight.

I stepped outside and watched, amazed that they were all imitating *me*. I remembered what that little boy told me after we had defeated the dragon—"You're the greatest superhero ever." I was pretty proud of myself for turning that dorky JuJu into a hero. Good thing I didn't pick a cool warrior, after all. We might have been dragon food.

"Eh, *almost* back to normal," the chancellor said, walking back inside.

That afternoon Katie came over, and we did something normal. We watched TV. No card games, no dimensions, no spells. Just plain old TV. Well, maybe I studied for an English test too. Now that Mom and Dad were so happy, I wanted it to stay that way.

"I don't think I've ever seen you study before," Katie said, cuddling Aidan.

"If JuJu can be the greatest superhero ever, then Joe can pass English," I concluded.

"Let's test each other," Katie said. "We each start with a hundred hitpoints. Every time one of us gets a question wrong, we lose twenty."

"Twenty?" I argued. "No way. Ten."

We ignored the TV and studied for the rest of the afternoon. When Mom and Dad came home, they were thrilled to see me doing schoolwork. They even helped quiz us before they grabbed Aidan and took him for a walk.

"How come I didn't think of this studying thing sooner?" I asked, staring at my English textbook with newfound confidence.

"Too bad you're out of hitpoints," Katie said, patting me on the cheek. "I win."

Before I could get angry, a red flash came from my textbook. A poem appeared, written in glowing red letters. It was called "A Formal Invitation." The first stanza read:

Come celebrate Komondor's newfound peace
And honor our legendary heroes.
If you're wondering where and when,
the answer is this:
Saturday night, at the floating palace!

Katie and I gave each other a wide-eyed glance, and then we eagerly read the rest of the poem.

That Saturday Dad came into my room carrying Aidan in one hand and a box in the other.

"I felt guilty that I threw out your fantasy toys, so I got you a gift," he said, handing me a computer game called *SesameQuest: Elmo and the Golden Lunchbox.* A caption on the box read "Learn to add while Elmo goes on an adventure!"

"Thanks, Dad," I said, adjusting my clip-on bowtie. "Maybe I'll play it tomorrow. Katie and I have a big date tonight." Dad suddenly looked like he swallowed the puppy.

When Katie arrived, I kicked Dad out of my room and put the Interdimensional Schlepp CD into my computer. We were immediately transported onto a floating glass platform surrounded by bright blue sky. Hundreds of well-dressed creatures milled around while Eryn and Kivin hovered over them in a small pod.

"There are *no* dwarfs on the menu, Guano," Bantam said. "For the last time, stop asking!"

"But Guano read invitation carefully," Guano said. "Invitation say that party have dwarfs for guests."

"It said that this party will *dwarf* all the rest!" Bantam squealed.

"Dis party be inimitable," the English Golem said, adjusting his tuxedo. "You two stops fighting or you spoils it." Myna flew overhead, carrying Mettyl, Fettyl, and Syzygy.

"I'm glad to see you got the invitation," JuJu said as he walked over to Katie and me. "Interdimensional messages can be so tricky."

"Attention, everyone! Attention, everyone!" Empress Grisette announced, clinking a glass with a spoon. "First I want to politely ask the thieves to stop stealing the silverware." Michael and his parents guiltily pulled a pile of forks and spoons out of their pockets and handed them back.

"Show everyone the dragon already!" Syzygy wailed.

"I commissioned an emerald plaque to be constructed in honor of the brave adventurers who restored peace to Komondor," Grisette continued. A palace servant pulled a sheet off of a mound, revealing a large green dragon covered with gold writing. "The plaque is made up of five separate

pieces, each containing part of the wonderful story."

"The prophecy cycle has ended!" Mettyl announced, pointing at the sky. Giant fireworks blasted overhead, causing bits of the glass platform to crack off. Eryn, Kivin, Katie, Michael, and I joined hands while the crowd showered us with confetti.

"To Komondor's heroes!" JuJu proclaimed, raising his staff in the air. The entire platform soared across the sky, looping around the palace a few times. During the chaos, Michael and the rest of the thieves slipped away.

"Two pieces of the DragonPlaque are missing!" Grisette observed after the crowd settled down.

"I will begin writing a new prophecy immediately," Syzygy said, reaching for a bottle of milk. "I suggest we scatter the remaining DragonPlaque pieces throughout Komondor and Earth to begin a new quest. I'll give the plaque the same divine power that the DragonSteel Amulet had, just to keep Komondor's tradition alive." Syzygy waved her hand, and the remaining pieces of the DragonPlaque glowed green. "The first stanza has already come to me." She took a quick swallow from her milk bottle and began reciting a poem:

A joyous party spoiled by thieves,

The fabled DragonPlaque stolen,
Its pieces scattered across Komondor and Earth—
What Chosen Ones will reunite them?

As the crowd applauded, Kivin emptied his velvet bag into the air, and a bunch of floating instruments began playing celebration music. All the guests danced at once.

"Look, Syzygy and the English Golem are dancing," Katie observed. "That's so cute!"

"Um, do I need to ask you to dance," I said nervously, "or is it just supposed to happen, like, naturally?"

Katie rolled her eyes and pulled me to the center of the dance floor.